Enter the
DARKNESS

ALSO BY SCOTT B. WILLIAMS

The Pulse
Refuge
Voyage After the Collapse
Landfall
The Darkness After
Into the River Lands
The Forge of Darkness
The Savage Darkness
Sailing the Apocalypse
On Island Time: Kayaking the Caribbean
Getting Out Alive
Exploring Coastal Mississippi
Bug Out
Bug Out Vehicles and Shelters

Copyright © 2017 by Scott B. Williams. All rights reserved. No part of this book may be reproduced or transmitted in any form or by any means, electronic or mechanical, including photocopying, recording, or by any information storage and retrieval system, without permission in writing from the author.

This is a work of fiction. Names, characters, places and events are all products of the author's imagination and should not be construed as real. Any resemblance to persons living or dead is purely coincidental.

ISBN-13: 978-1544266411
Cover photograph: © Scott B. Williams
Cover and interior design: Scott B. Williams
Editors: Michelle Cleveland, Bill Barker

Enter the DARKNESS
Darkness After Series

Scott B. Williams

This one is for Frank & Cathy,

Preface

I WROTE *THE DARKNESS After* in 2013 on contract with the same publishing company that published *The Pulse: A Novel of Surviving the Collapse of the Grid*, as well as some of my nonfiction titles prior to that. *The Pulse* was so successful upon its release in June of 2012 that the publisher asked me to write *The Darkness After* as a parallel story set in the same world, but with younger characters and targeted at the Young Adult audience. Both books turned out to be popular, and my readers were soon asking if there would be sequels. At the time of this writing, each of those books is now a four-book series with more sequels in the works.

This 36,000-word prequel novella, *Enter the Darkness*—is another entry point into the *Darkness After Series* for new readers and provides a bit of backstory for those of you who have read all the later books. Some of the scenes in *Enter the Darkness* were cut from the first-draft manuscript of *The Darkness After* because of length restraints. In the revision process at the time, I decided to jump right in with the first action scene where Mitch Henley meets April Gibbs on the

ENTER THE DARKNESS

road, rather than tell the story beginning with the occurrence of the EMP event.

This prequel goes back and fills in the gap, beginning with Mitch getting stuck on a busy New Orleans street when his dad's new pickup suddenly goes dead at a red light. It also tells the story of the worst day in April Gibbs' life—the morning she wakes up to learn that her child is stranded more than a hundred miles away from home. What she decides to do at that point leads to her fortuitous meeting with Mitch, who happens to have the means and ability to help her out of a dire predicament. *Enter the Darkness* also gives you a glimpse of how those first days play out for April's boyfriend, David Greene, and Mitch's little sister, Lisa Henley.

The Darkness After Series can certainly be read without this prequel, but those of you who have read the other books might enjoy learning a little more about the main characters and who they were before their lives changed forever with the collapse of the grid. For those readers who have not read any of the other books in the series, *Enter the Darkness* is probably the best place to start to get the full story from the beginning.

I'm often asked how likely it is that such a powerful solar flare could occur, and whether or not I think the effects could be as devastating as I portray them in these stories. The answer is that scientists who study these things say that it *is* possible, and even *probable*, because it *has* happened before, just not since civilization has become so dependent upon vulnerable electronics technology. No one can predict for certain when such a solar event may occur, but many of those who study the subject have advised government planning and preparation for such a catastrophe, including measures to harden the grid infrastructure to better withstand the effects.

As for the human impacts of such a disaster, I only know what I saw in the wake of a far lesser event—*Hurricane Katrina*—when the grid in my local region was down for several weeks and people were stranded without the essentials for survival. It doesn't take a great imagination to see how things would play out if a complete blackout of power, communications, and transportation were to occur across an entire continent and beyond. The darkness would manifest in more ways than the obvious; and regrettably for many, in the darker side of human nature.

This series of stories is meant to be fun and entertaining for both Young Adult and older readers, but be warned that it is also at times violent and perhaps a bit frightening in its portrayal of the savagery to which some would undoubtedly resort in the absence of all law and order.

Scott B. Williams —March 2017

One

MITCH HENLEY HATED JUST about everything about cities, but the thing he hated the most was the traffic. He swore under his breath as he inched his dad's new F-150 along at ten miles per hour, glad to finally be moving, even at that excruciating pace. He had been stuck on I-610 trying to get out of New Orleans for over an hour. Something had happened far up ahead that he couldn't yet see, no doubt a major accident considering how long it was taking to clear it. He looked around him at all the frustrated commuters who had to deal with this stuff on a daily basis, and was thankful that at least he was headed *out* of the city. He couldn't wait to cross the bridge over Lake Pontchartrain, and soon after, the Mississippi state line.

Back there, in the rural county where he lived, he'd been driving around the farm and on the quiet local country roads since long before he was old enough to get his license. He was 16 now and fully legal, but his experience driving in heavy traffic was still quite limited. Mitch had confidence in his abilities and was a careful and considerate driver; but it

ENTER THE DARKNESS

was obvious many of those around him were not. He was glad for the heavy-duty cattle guard on the front of the new Ford, but he really hoped he wouldn't need it before he reached the open highway.

Now that the traffic was at least crawling, Mitch realized he needed to look for an exit so he could find a bathroom. Out in the country, he could stop nearly anywhere along the side of the road if there wasn't a convenient gas station or store. Here, even if he managed to get off the expressway, he would have to sit through stoplights to get to a store or restaurant that had both public restrooms and adequate parking. Then he would have to fight his way back the same way and merge into the traffic all over again. He couldn't wait until he reached Slidell though, as he had no way of knowing how long that would take with so many drivers delayed by the accident. He nudged his way back into the right lane at the first opportunity and stayed there until he saw the billboard for a popular fast-food chain. It would cost him another half hour, but he figured he could get some breakfast while he was there and maybe by then the congestion would have cleared.

Sitting at the first stoplight off the exit, Mitch looked at his watch—nearly 8 a.m. already. He had dropped his mom and dad off at the airport at just before 6:00, and their flight was supposed to leave at 6:50. They were probably landing in Houston by now, and would soon make their connection on to Denver. His mom said she would call as soon as they were on the ground, and he expected to hear from her any minute. He turned down the music so he wouldn't miss his ringtone and stared at the traffic light, willing it to switch from red to green. Like everything else to do with driving in the city, Mitch hated the red lights—especially the ones that took forever to change. He was fast losing his patience when he noticed it suddenly blink and go completely off. When it flashed back on a couple of times it was still red, and then it went out completely.

It took him a moment to realize it, but the radio in the truck went silent at the same time the traffic light blinked off. In the absence of the music, the engine seemed quieter than normal too, although at idle it was so quiet anyway it was hard to be sure it was running. He took his foot off the brake to inch forward and make sure, but nothing happened, not even when he gently tapped the accelerator. The engine had apparently gone dead, but that was a ridiculous idea considering the F-150 was literally *brand new*. His father had just traded for it less than two weeks ago. Mitch tried restarting it, expecting immediate results, but there was nothing—no sound of the motor turning over or even the click of the starter relay. Then he noticed that the digital indicators on the dash were out just like the radio. It appeared that the vehicle's electrical system had completely failed, and he had no idea what could cause that unless it was something to do with the battery.

ENTER THE DARKNESS

Nervous at the thought of being stalled in all that traffic, Mitch glanced at the light again, certain it would be green by now and surprised that people behind him weren't already blasting their horns for him to get out of the way. But the light wasn't green *or* red; it was still simply out, and no one around him seemed to be moving either. The truck still wouldn't start when he tried it again, so Mitch pulled the hood latch under the dash and opened his door. As he stepped down from the cab and walked to the front of the truck, he was so focused on figuring out what was wrong with his dad's truck that at first he didn't notice the other drivers exiting their vehicles as well. He lifted the hood and looked for loose wires or other clues like smoke, but didn't see or smell anything unusual under there. He tugged on the battery cable connections to make sure they were still tight, but they seemed fine. He was sure it was an electrical problem but he couldn't find anything obviously amiss. By the time he'd checked everything he knew to look for, he finally noticed that many of the other people stopped in the street around him seemed to be having problems too.

A cab driver on the other side of the intersection slammed his hood shut and kicked his front tire as he cursed his stalled car. An exasperated woman standing behind the open car door of her SUV was pressing on her phone and shaking it as if she were trying to get it to work. The middle-aged man who'd been at the wheel of the Lexus sedan behind

Mitch was walking towards him now, not to yell at him for blocking the road, but with a look of bewilderment on his face.

"Is yours dead too?" he asked.

"Yeah. Nothing's working, not even the instrument panel, it's like the battery just died."

"Mine too. I wonder what in the heck is going on? How could so many people have the same problem at once?" The man was taking in the scene around the intersection, where most of the nearby vehicles were sitting still, with their hoods up. Mitch noticed that people were coming out of nearby businesses too and gathering on the sidewalks. It was then that he noticed that none of those buildings had lights visible through their windows, nor were any outside signs lit. The power was apparently off, and that explained the traffic light going out, but what did that have to do with his truck and all these other stalled vehicles in the street?

He was about to reply that it didn't make any sense when the sound of a tremendous explosion from somewhere in the near distance caused him to flinch in surprise. The nearest buildings on that side of the street blocked the view in the direction from which the blast had seemed to come, but people across the street were pointing that way and screaming about a plane crash.

"It just flew straight into the ground!" one woman yelled.

Those that had seen it were all pointing to the west,

ENTER THE DARKNESS

which Mitch knew was the direction to the airport. Before he could give it further thought there was more yelling about another one and Mitch had just enough time to catch a glimpse of a jumbo jet in the skies to the north of them that appeared to be losing altitude at an alarming rate.

"It's going down in the lake!" someone screamed.

Mitch knew the vast expanse of Lake Pontchartrain lay in that direction, but the buildings and elevated roadway hid any view of the water from where he stood. He stood mesmerized as the plane headed nearly straight down until it was lost from sight beyond the elevated I-610 Expressway he'd been traveling earlier. There was no doubt it crashed into the water somewhere far out in the lake, and he suddenly remembered he was waiting on a call from his mother and that he'd left his cell phone on the seat of the truck. He quickly jerked the door open and grabbed it. His mom should have called by now, and he might have missed her while he was standing outside the truck. But when he checked to see if there had been an incoming call, all he saw was a dead screen. The phone didn't light up when he pressed the home button to wake it, and even when he tried to restart it nothing happened. Now he was really confused. *What could possibly knock out the power and cause vehicles and phones to go dead at the same time? And did it whatever it was also cause those two planes to crash?*

The thought made him sick with worry over his mom and

dad, but he reminded himself their plane was hundreds of miles away approaching Houston, if it not already on the ground, which it probably was. Mitch checked his watch again, noting that the minute hand showed that it was now almost 10 minutes after 8:00. At least the watch was working. It was an old-school analog model rather than the high-tech digital variety most people wore, if they wore one at all in an age of smart phones in every pocket or purse.

Looking at the scene around him again, Mitch saw that many of the stranded commuters were virtually in a state of panic. Most had abandoned their stalled vehicles and were walking or running to the nearby buildings. He heard one man yelling something about a terrorist attack and saw the effect it had on the crowd. No doubt the sight of airplanes falling from the sky brought back memories of television footage Mitch had seen many years after that terrible day, when he was old enough to understand. But how could terrorists cause all of these cars and trucks to suddenly go dead? There *had* to be a reasonable explanation for it, and Mitch was determined to stay calm and try to figure it out. He spotted the man he'd first talked to from the car behind him and walked across the street to where he was standing on the sidewalk with his own phone in hand, apparently trying to get his to work again too. Mitch knew the man was as baffled as everyone else, but at least he was probably from around here and Mitch was so out of his element that talking to a local

ENTER THE DARKNESS

seemed like the best thing he could do at the moment.

Two

APRIL GIBBS OPENED HER eyes and was instantly wide-awake at the sight of sunlight streaming through her bedroom window. She jumped up in disbelief, furious because she had to be at work by 8:30 and it had to be after 8:00 already. *Where was David and why didn't he wake her up at seven like he was supposed to?* She stormed out of the bedroom calling his name but got no response. He wasn't in the apartment and looking out the front window, she saw that her car wasn't parked out front either.

April went back to the bedroom for her phone, yanking it free of the charger before heading to the bathroom. She was going to call David Greene and let him have it. *How could anyone nearly 20-years-old be so irresponsible? And why had she been stupid enough to have a child with him?* David had to be at work this morning too, and it was nearly a two-hour drive from Hattiesburg to New Orleans. He had her car because once again, his "classic" Mustang wasn't running, but he had promised to be home with their daughter no later than seven.

April pressed the home button on her phone to wake it

ENTER THE DARKNESS

up. When nothing happened she assumed it had powered down, even though she *never* turned it off intentionally. She knew it had a full charge because it had been plugged in all night. But try as she might, she couldn't get the display to come on. She tried rebooting it to no avail. Then she shook it vigorously and tapped it hard against the heel of her palm. Nothing seemed to jar it back to life. *Great! Now I'm not only going to be late for work, I can't even call in and let Vanessa know!*

April flipped the switch to the bathroom light but nothing happened. The light didn't come on. *Really? Could so many different little things really conspire against her in one freakin' morning?* She made her way to the kitchen to get a bulb out of the cabinet over the sink and was surprised to discover that the light in there wasn't working either. It didn't seem possible that two bulbs in two separate rooms could burn out simultaneously, so she began to suspect something else was up even before she confirmed it by glancing at the digital clock on the stove and seeing that it too was out. She opened the fridge and found it dark inside. *So, the power went out overnight.* That could explain why her phone was dead. She had run it nearly down the night before playing music, so if the charger wasn't getting power while she slept the battery could have completely drained before morning. Now she had no way to charge it, since she didn't even have her car and the 12-volt charger she always kept in the console. She would have to catch a cab to get to work, but without the phone she couldn't even call one. She and David didn't have a landline in the little apartment because they didn't see a need for it and couldn't afford another utility bill anyway.

It made no sense that the power would go out in perfectly good weather, so April figured it wasn't storm related, but probably some kind of maintenance issue. Whatever it was, it didn't matter. She had to get to work and *now*. Whenever David finally got back he was going to have to take Kimberly to daycare before he could go to his own job. She should have known better than to let him take her car out of town on a work night, but there hadn't been much of a choice. David's parents had been keeping Kimberly for the weekend, and she had been unable to go and pick her up Monday morning, her normal day off, because a coworker called in sick and she had a class to attend that evening. So Kimberly got an extra night with her grandma and grandpa and David got a Monday night road trip in April's car. If she knew David, he'd probably gone out to look up some of his old high school buddies as soon as Kimberly was put to bed. That would explain why he'd slept in and neglected to even call her, much less make it back to New Orleans before she had to leave for work. He was going to get a piece of her mind when she got home tonight, that was for sure. April had about enough of David Greene already, and she doubted they were going to make it much longer. Knowing this made her glad they hadn't officially tied the knot. They'd planned to at

ENTER THE DARKNESS

one time, but the longer they were together the less it seemed like a good idea. He had come into her life at a vulnerable time, shortly after she lost her mother after already losing her father a few years before. David had been kind and caring then, and they seemed to have a lot in common until they actually started living together. But he was immature and not ready for the responsibilities of fatherhood. April figured she would end up raising Kimberly alone, and she was prepared to do it if that was the way it worked out.

She finished dressing and went back to the kitchen to leave a note for him. She desperately needed a cup of coffee, but of course, the coffee maker was useless too and it would have to wait until she got to work. She locked the door and descended the steps to the sidewalk to get around the railing separating their half of the converted duplex from the neighbor's. Mrs. Landry was an elderly widow who was usually home, and always up early, so April didn't hesitate to knock on her door to ask if she could use her landline. She needed to call a cab and she needed to do it soon. She was already going to be late, and she couldn't afford to get fired. Mrs. Landry was hard of hearing, so April pounded louder to get her to the door.

"It's not working, sweetie," the elderly woman said when she finally opened it and heard April's request. "I tried to call my sister, Julie in Slidell to see if their power was out on the North Shore too, and I couldn't get a dial tone. The power and the phone lines are both out, so it seems."

"Well rats! I don't know how I'm going to get to work then. David's got my car and he was supposed to be back early this morning with Kimberly, but I haven't seen or heard from him."

"He may have a problem with the car, sweetie. Look over there across the street at Jennifer's house. I heard her slamming doors earlier and looked out to see that she couldn't seem to get her car started. The hood's been up for half an hour and she's gone back inside. And I haven't seen *any* cars drive by since the power went off."

That kind of coincidence didn't mean much to April, but she was curious to know when the blackout happened. "You mean it went off sometime after you got up this morning?"

"Oh yes, dear. It was just a few minutes before eight. It hasn't been all that long."

"That's odd," April said. "I figured it happened right after I went to bed, because my iPhone was completely dead when I got up. But if the power was still on all night, it should have gotten a full charge long before it went out."

"I don't know much about those things, but I do know that it's unusual for the old-fashioned telephones like mine to go out. That never happens in a power outage."

"I'm going to walk over there and see what's going on with Jennifer's car and see if she knows anything about all this. I'll let you know if I find out anything."

ENTER THE DARKNESS

April was beyond frustrated and getting worried too. On the one hand, she was upset thinking David had stayed out late and overslept this morning, but now she wondered if his being late was somehow related to what was going on here. Either way, she was stranded with no way to get to work and she couldn't call him to check on Kimberly.

She didn't really know Jennifer, but the 30-something divorcee that lived alone in the house across the street always seemed friendly enough, waving whenever she saw April pushing Kimberly along the sidewalk in her stroller. When she came to the door, Jennifer seemed glad to see her, as if she thought April might have some answers. When April told her she was just as baffled as everyone else, Jennifer walked out to the white Buick with her to show her what it was doing. The interior lights still came on when she opened the door, but turning the key did nothing. The starter didn't spin and April didn't even hear the small humming sound that David had told her was the fuel pump when she asked him about it in her own car.

"I've never had a problem with this car since I've owned it," Jennifer said. "It's always been serviced at the dealership where I bought it and it's still under warranty. I would call them to come pick it up, but there's no way to call. I guess I'll just have to wait until the power and phones come back on."

April heard what she was saying, but she was busy scanning what she could see of the rest of the neighborhood at the same time. Something seemed really weird, and it took her a minute to realize that it was the *quiet*. She had never heard the city so quiet. The background noise of traffic that could normally be heard from every direction was *gone*. The underlying hum of other unseen machinery and power lines and who knew what else was missing too. Those sounds were all replaced by the voices of people talking or calling out to each other, the opening and closing of doors and birdcalls and squirrel chatter from the branches overhead that shaded the street. Something really strange was going on, and April was beginning to sense it was more than just a power outage, especially when she learned that Jennifer's cell phone was as dead as her own.

"It was working when I got up at my usual time around 6:30. I had my coffee while I was reading for a few minutes, and it was still working the last time I looked at it before I went to get a shower before work. The lights went out while I was in there, and when I came out to dry off, I discovered the phone was dead too. That was before I even tried to start the car. What could make our cell phones go out like that?"

"I don't know," April said, "but I'm going to take a walk around the block and ask around. There's got to be someone who might know."

"That sounds like a good idea. I'd go with you but I'd probably just slow you down. Please tell me if you find out anything though."

ENTER THE DARKNESS

"I will," April promised. And with that she headed for the street, turning east in the direction where she'd heard most of the voices.

Three

THE MAN FROM THE Lexus looked up from the phone that had been the sole focus of his attention until he noticed Mitch's approach. "Darned thing has gone into brick mode apparently. What about yours? Any luck?

"Nope. Mine did the same thing. It doesn't make any sense. I'm Mitch Henley, by the way," Mitch said, extending his hand.

"Charles Greenfield. Pleased to meet you Mitch. That's a nice new Ford truck you're driving, and I noticed your Mississippi plates...."

Mitch could tell the fifty-something-year-old man was probably wondering how a kid his age could afford such an expensive truck. "Yeah, it's my dad's. He just bought it a couple of weeks ago. I had to drive him and my mom down to the airport this morning. That's why I was wondering about your phone. I need to call them and make sure they're okay. They should be in Houston already, but I'm worried about them now after those two plane crashes."

"I'm sure whatever caused those two crashes isn't

ENTER THE DARKNESS

affecting anything as far away as Houston, but I can understand your concern. That's the main reason I've been trying to get this blasted phone to work. I was hoping to find some news online that might give us a clue about what's going on, but no such luck. It's all really bizarre, I'll grant you that. First all these cars going dead.... then planes crashing.... the power going out and our phones dying too...." Mr. Greenfield looked bewildered, but he was still calmer than most of those around them, many of whom were in full manic mode by now.

"It had to all happen at the same time, right? I mean, just when I noticed that stoplight go out was when the radio went out in the truck. I just didn't realize the engine was dead at first because these new ones are so quiet compared to what I'm used to. Whatever it was that knocked out the power must have fried the electronics in our vehicles and phones.... and in those airplanes. Those jets can't fly without their electronic controls, can they?"

"I don't think so, no. But you're right. It's got to be something electrical-related." Mr. Greenfield stared at the inert smartphone in the palm of his hand as he talked. "It's like the way a lightning strike knocks out the power. But whoever heard of a lightning strike with enough energy to take out the circuitry in cars and airplanes?

"It probably could in a direct hit," Mitch said. "I've seen it blow an oak tree into toothpicks, but I don't think lightning did this. There's not a cloud in the sky and I haven't heard any thunder, have you?"

"No. Of course it wasn't really lighting, but I have no idea what else could have done it. And I wonder how big an area it affected. Those planes went down at least several miles away."

"That's what has me worried. If I can't call, I can't be sure my mom and dad are okay just because they're supposed to be in Houston."

"Maybe there's a land line in one of those stores you could use. Land lines don't go out when the power goes off."

"Yeah, you're right. That's a good idea! I got off on this exit in the first place because I needed to find a restroom. They probably have a phone in that convenience store," Mitch said, pointing to the gas station and store across the street at the next intersection.

"Mind if I walk along with you?" I should try to call my office downtown anyway. It looks like I'm going to be late for an important appointment."

"Sure," Mitch said. "I just want to lock up the truck first. I guess no one will mind if we park where we are," he laughed, trying to lighten the mood and put the worry out of his mind, if only for a moment.

"I should guess not, but if they do, they'll have a lot more tickets to write besides just our two," Mr. Greenfield said, looking around as they worked their way through the dozens of stalled vehicles in the immediate vicinity. Farther away, it

ENTER THE DARKNESS

looked like the same situation on every bit of roadway they could see. The interstate overpass to the north was strangely silent, the big semi trucks and commuter cars alike all immobilized wherever they had come to a stop when their engines stalled.

"Where in Mississippi do you live, Mitch? My wife and I get over to Biloxi pretty often."

"It's out in the middle of nowhere. Well to the east of Interstate 59 and Highway 49, over in Stone County. If you've ever heard of Black Creek, our land is really close to it."

"It seems to ring a bell."

"You would have crossed a bridge over it if you ever went to Hattiesburg from the Gulf Coast on 49."

"That's probably where I saw the name then."

"Do you live in New Orleans?" Mitch asked.

"Metairie actually, not far from here on the Lakeshore. But my office is downtown, right off Canal."

"Wow, it's gotta suck to drive through this traffic here everyday. I was stuck on 610 for nearly an hour this morning because of a wreck. What kind of work do you do down there?"

"I'm an attorney. I don't mind the traffic really. It's not *that* bad most of the time. I understand how you feel though. I grew up in the country too, on a big farm in Iowa. I left there when I wasn't much older than you and never looked back. I love it here in the Big Easy, but I've got to admit, this is the weirdest thing I've seen happen here. The lights were out for a long time after Hurricane Katrina hit, but we were away on vacation at the time, so I missed the worst of that."

They reached the convenience store and found all the employees and customers standing around outside or in the doorways. No, the landline phone in the store didn't work, according to the manager. Yes, they could go in and use the bathroom, but it was pitch-dark back there because there were no windows to let in daylight. Mitch had a mini-flashlight on his keychain though, so he managed to find his way to the men's room without issue. When he made his way back outside, Mr. Greenfield was waiting by the door.

"You know, this is really a lot worse than I thought it was at first," Mr. Greenfield said as they walked back out into the parking lot. One of the customers that had been in there when it first happened was talking about a possible EMP event. He said he saw strange lights in the sky after midnight last night, and that maybe it was a strong solar flare that caused this."

"A solar flare?" Mitch looked at Mr. Greenfield as it dawned on him that this idea made a lot more sense than anything else he could think of. He'd seen a cable TV documentary about solar flares, and how scientists agreed that a really powerful one could destroy the complex technology grid everyone was so dependent upon. A big

ENTER THE DARKNESS

enough electromagnetic pulse generated by a strong solar flare could essentially shut down all of our power and communication systems. At least that was the theory.

"I don't know why I didn't think about that before, Mitch. I've read about solar EMPs somewhere, but just never thought much of it. The idea seemed rather far-fetched, to be honest."

"I rarely watch TV, but Dad and my sister had it on one of the science channels one night and I sat down for a few minutes to see what the show was about. Some guy was talking about how NASA was concerned that we were overdue for a major solar flare, and that if a big enough one occurred, it could disrupt everything on Earth. At the time, I thought that might be a good thing, because you know, no more *school!*"

Mr. Greenfield chuckled at this, but then began to wonder. "I could see how the power grid and the cell networks would be affected. But man, it would have to be some kind of powerful to interfere with airplanes and car engines."

"They said it would be; that there would be so much voltage or current or whatever that it would just fry all that stuff and wipe out most of our technology. Dad always said these newer cars and trucks were too complicated and you can't even work on them anymore. Everything about them is controlled by little black boxes that are really computers."

"Yes, of course. That's true. I can see the vulnerability, but it's so strange to think that something you can't hear, or see, or even feel could unleash that much destructive power."

"But you said someone saw lights in the sky last night?"

"Yes. But that was hours before. Nothing happened last night though, as far as I know."

"Well, maybe there was another, *stronger* solar flare this morning, and the reason we couldn't see anything was because it happened in the daylight, and well after sunrise at that. That could explain it, couldn't it?"

"I suppose so. Yes, that's got to be it!"

"On that TV show this one scientist who studies them said major solar flares have hit the Earth before. There was a big one sometime in the late 1800s that affected things in the northeast and up in Canada. But back then there wasn't much for it to destroy like there is now. He said they probably occurred many times before that too, but no one would have noticed the effects back before they had electricity. Now that everything runs on computers and electronics, it's far worse. This could turn out to be *really* bad, Mr. Greenfield. He said a strong enough solar event could wipe out civilization as we know it!"

The two of them walked back to where they'd left their stalled vehicles as they talked. Mitch was deep in thought as he pondered the implications of their discussion. If what they were speculating was correct, then the impact of the

ENTER THE DARKNESS

event would be far reaching—affecting an untold area well beyond the city of New Orleans—and maybe even beyond the entire southeastern United States. It could have affected the whole country, or for that matter, the world. Surely if it was powerful enough to wipe out everything electrical here, it would have done the same in Houston, only a few hundred miles to the west. Mitch could only hope his mom and dad were safely stranded at the airport there, and that they had not been in flight when this mysterious pulse occurred. But how would he *know?* The more he thought about it, the more he began to realize that there probably wasn't any way he would, at least not immediately. He couldn't get through to them by any means, nor could he drive there to see. And likewise, they couldn't call him or his sister, Lisa, or easily return to New Orleans or to their farm in Mississippi. The one thing Mitch *could* do though was go home. And he knew he had to, because his little sister was going to need him until after all this confusion was cleared up and the power came back on.

Four

LISA HENLEY RARELY GOT the opportunity to spend a school night at Stacy's house, but she loved that she could sleep in a half hour later there than she could at home. Instead of a 20-minute early morning ride into town with her brother, school was just a short walk down the street from where Stacy lived. What was even better was that Stacy's mom worked nights at the hospital in Hattiesburg, so the two girls could get away with staying up as late as they wanted. Jason was supposed to make sure they went to bed at a decent hour, but he didn't really care. He had spent the evening shut in his room with his electric guitar, the amp blasting as loud as Stacy would tolerate without beating on his door and screaming. Mitch could be obnoxious too, but Lisa was glad he preferred to go off hunting in the woods instead of making racket at home like Stacy's older brother.

Even though they had to put up with Jason, it was great fun for Lisa to get a break from her routine and spend the night hanging out with Stacy. They stayed up until nearly 2 a.m., talking and watching TV shows her mom and dad would

ENTER THE DARKNESS

never allow her to see at home. Both of them were up in time to get ready for school though, and even Jason finally emerged after Stacy's relentless efforts to wake him.

"I wish I could just stay here the rest of the week," Lisa told Stacy, as they sat at the table with their bowls of cereal.

"I don't see why you can't. Your mom and dad won't be back until Friday. Why do they want you to go back home with Mitch after school today anyway?"

"So I can do my stupid chores. They said it wasn't fair to Mitch to have to do them all every day they're gone, especially since he had to drive them to New Orleans."

"Yeah, like *that* was a chore! He gets to spend half the day driving your dad's brand new truck *and* skipping school at the same time."

"I know. I just wish I had my license. If I did, I could have driven them there, and I would have spent the rest of the day hanging out in New Orleans. Mitch hates the city though. He'll drive straight back as fast as he can just so he can go hunting the rest of the day."

"I don't get it. He can hunt any time. Doesn't he want to do something different once in a while?"

"No, not Mitch. He's just boring like that."

"If he can get back here in time to hunt, he could make it to most of his classes too."

"Yeah, like he cares about *that*. Mitch would have already quit school if Mom and Dad would let him. You know that."

"Has Mom called this morning?" Jason asked as he came in the kitchen to get his breakfast, his hair still wet from the shower.

"No, but she ought to be here any minute now. It's almost a quarter 'til eight."

"I hope so. I need to borrow ten bucks from her. Mr. Calloway is going to Hattiesburg after music class today and he said he would pick up a set of strings for me if I gave him the money."

"Mom's gonna say you don't need them. Why *do* you need them? The ones you've got sounded like they were working last night."

"They're dead, that's why. Bending the notes playing lead wears them out."

"Yeah, *whatever.*"

Stacy wasn't impressed with her brother's playing, and after hearing his latest efforts last night, Lisa could see why. It was the same old Led Zeppelin song over and over for what must have been hours, never quite right, but loud enough that there was no escaping it in the small wood-frame house.

Five more minutes passed by the time they were done with breakfast and Stacy's mom still wasn't home. There wasn't enough time to wait any longer since it appeared they were going to have to walk to school, so Jason locked the house, grumbling about not having the extra ten bucks he needed.

ENTER THE DARKNESS

"I can loan it to you," Lisa said. "But you're going to have to pay me back tomorrow. I've got just enough lunch money to last me through Friday." She handed him the money and Jason stuck it in his pocket before trying to call their mom again as they walked.

"Hey, this is weird! My phone just shut down right when I tried to make a call."

"Probably because you forgot to charge it," his little sister said.

"I didn't forget. It had a full battery just before we left the house."

"Did you try turning it back on?" Lisa asked.

"Of course I did. I'm not stupid! I'm still trying now. Nothing's happening though."

"I guess you're out of luck then. Maybe it'll come back on by itself later."

"Yeah, it could be doing an automatic update or something," Lisa said. She didn't have her own phone, because her mom and dad didn't think she needed one until she was old enough to drive. Stacy's mom felt the same. Both of them had older brothers who did carry phones and if they were anywhere they might need to call home from, they were likely with their brothers or another adult.

As they made their way closer to the school, walking along the main road where the parents who drove their children dropped them off, Lisa noticed several vehicles stopped in random places in the middle of the road. People were getting out of them and there were also more students than usual standing around outside the building when it was time to get to class. As they got closer, they could see even more students coming out and none going inside. Something out of the ordinary was going on.

"Hey what's up, Michael?" Jason asked, when they were close enough to call out to one of his friends.

"The lights just went out; right after I got here. Looks like there won't be any first period class today, man!"

"Dang it! I could've slept in! I wish I'd known sooner!"

Lisa and Stacy left Jason there talking to Michael and some more of his friends and walked the rest of the way to the sidewalk where some of their own classmates were gathered. It only took a few minutes to learn that the problem was bigger than just an ordinary power outage. Everyone they talked to who had a cell phone said that theirs had suddenly shut down, just like Jason's did. And the stalled cars and pickups on the road out front went dead at the same time. The teachers and other adults outside didn't have an explanation for it, and seemed just as confused and surprised as the students. The power went out fairly often at her house and even here at the school when there were bad thunderstorms, but it was a clear, sunny morning today, and Lisa didn't see how it could be weather related. No one else seemed to know either. Lisa saw her science teacher talking to

ENTER THE DARKNESS

the principle outside of his office, and urged Stacy to go with her to ask him if he had any ideas.

"Maybe Mr. Smith will know what happened," she said.

"I hope so. I just heard Cara Anderson saying something crazy about how aliens might have caused it. She said there were weird lights in the sky last night, and that her brother thinks they were UFOs. He said if aliens were attacking the Earth, they would probably do something just like this; use some kind of force to zap all our electronic devices and vehicles so we'll be helpless."

"That sounds like something from a stupid B movie. Her brother watches too much cable TV."

"Maybe. But this *is* really weird, don't you think?"

"Of course it is. But there's got to be an explanation. I'll bet Mr. Smith has an idea. He knows so much about everything."

They stood patiently waiting until their teacher finished his conversation with the principle, then Lisa asked him what he thought had happened.

"I don't have enough information yet to know for sure, but I'm afraid this could be the result of a strong electromagnetic pulse. There's really nothing else that would explain it."

"Electromagnetic pulse?" Stacy asked. "What exactly is that?"

"A strong surge caused by solar activity, most likely. I've

read quite a few articles in the science journals recently speculating that we've been overdue for a powerful solar event that could have an impact on our technology. It's happened before, but not since civilization was so dependent upon the power grid."

"Cara Anderson said there were weird lights in the sky late last night. We didn't see any because we were inside."

"No, I didn't see them either, but Mr. Denton said a few people told him they did. That's why I think it was a solar flare. It can cause visible effects like that. It looks a lot like the Aurora Borealis, which we almost never get to see at this latitude."

"But if it happened last night, then why did the power go off just now, right before school started?" Lisa wanted to know.

"The lights people saw last night were probably from a much smaller solar flare that occurred first. They usually occur in series. The one that caused the damage today was far stronger. We wouldn't have seen the lights because the sun was already up and the sky too bright, but I'll bet they were visible farther west, especially on the West Coast, since they're two hours behind us."

"Would it really affect places that far away the same as it did here?"

"Oh yes, definitely. Let's just hope the results were not as devastating elsewhere as they apparently were here. This

ENTER THE DARKNESS

could be an unprecedented disaster if it's as bad as some scientists have predicated such a pulse could be."

"Well I didn't feel anything," Stacy said. "It doesn't look like anybody got hurt, and it didn't start any fires or anything like that, at least not that we can see. It must not be *so* bad. They'll just have to fix the power lines and people may have to get new cell phones. How is that really a disaster?"

"What about cars?" Lisa interrupted. "They went dead too. What's up with that?"

"They stopped running because just about all the vehicles on the road today depend on multiple electronic components to operate," Mr. Smith said. "But to answer Stacy's question; this is really bad because all the things that probably were damaged can't be fixed without replacement parts and a means to get them where they're needed. That includes things like transformers that are essential to the power grid, but that's not even the real problem. The *real* problem is that communications could be down all over the country. People everywhere will be isolated and cut off, and stores will run out of food and other essentials if the trucks are not running to bring in more. You know how it is when a hurricane hits the Gulf Coast. Now imagine one big enough to affect the entire United States, and you will begin to get the idea."

"So I guess we're not going to be having class today," Stacy said. "Can we go home then? My mom wasn't back this morning when she was supposed to be, and now I'm worried about her. What if her car stopped on the highway somewhere along the way?"

"I think we're going to dismiss everyone shortly," Mr. Smith said. "I know you live close enough to walk home, Stacy, but if you do, you need to go straight there and stay put. Do you know where your father is working today, Lisa? I'm sure all the law enforcement agencies are going to do whatever they can to get some information and assist anyone they can."

"He had to go to Colorado with my mom for a funeral. Their plane was leaving this morning, and Mitch drove them to the airport. I spent the night with Stacy because of that."

Lisa saw by the look on Mr. Smith's face that he thought that was bad news. Did it mean her mom and dad wouldn't be able to come back on Friday because of all this? She looked around her at all the confusion and wondered what was going to happen next. Then it occurred to her that Mitch might be stranded too. If he was still in New Orleans, he was going to be furious, because he hated cities with a passion. She didn't know what she was going to do if he didn't return when he was supposed to. All she could do for now was stick with Stacy and Jason until they all found out more.

Five

DAVID GREENE KNEW HE'D had far too many beers to be driving. He'd already gotten one DUI in Hattiesburg the summer after he graduated high school. He couldn't afford another, so he decided the smart thing to do would be to crash on Josh's couch and go pick up Kimberly early in the morning. His mom and dad's house wasn't far from his buddy's apartment, so he figured he'd have plenty of time to stop by to get his daughter and still make it to New Orleans with April's car in time for her to get to work.

"Hey man, my phone's almost dead and I don't have my charger. Can you set your alarm for like 4:30 and make sure I'm up? I told April I would be back home by seven, but it'll be cool as long as I'm no more than a half hour late. She'll still have time to get to work."

"Sure, dude. I'll get you up."

David wasn't in a state of mind to be too concerned about tomorrow when he passed out on the couch. He didn't get to hang out with Josh very often, so they'd made the most of it while they had the chance. The Bud Light bottles lined

ENTER THE DARKNESS

up in neat rows on the coffee table were evidence of that. The next thing he was aware of was someone pushing on his shoulder, shaking him awake. When David opened his eyes and saw that it was no longer dark in the apartment living room, he knew he had screwed up big time.

"What time is it, Josh?"

"A little after seven-thirty. Sorry man, but I forgot to set the alarm. Hey, I've got to go right now. I'm gonna be late for work already."

David stumbled to his feet and looked around the room for his shoes. April was going to be furious, but she would have to deal with it. He didn't feel like hearing it right now, so he wasn't about to call her, especially with his head throbbing from a hangover. He would run home to his parent's house as fast as he could get there and grab Kimberly, and then he would call her from the road once he was on the way. There would definitely be a major fight over this but it wouldn't be the first one and he knew it wouldn't be the last. If he had been able to come here in the Mustang, it wouldn't be an issue because April could go on to work and he could drop Kimberly off at day care himself. He would have it running again soon, at least that's what he kept telling himself, because all he had to do was rebuild the carburetor. Then he'd be riding in style instead of begging April for the use of her stupid little Honda.

Unlike his antique Ford though, the Honda never broke

down or missed a beat. At least it never *had*, until this very morning when he was just two block's from his parent's house and it suddenly went dead as he slowed for a stop sign. He couldn't get it started again and after getting out for a look, he figured it was an electrical problem rather than a fuel issue. Slamming the hood in disgust, David jogged the rest of the way to the house. He didn't have time to fool with the car until he at least called April to tell her what was going on. But now that he had car trouble, he had a legitimate excuse for being late so he wouldn't have to make one up.

"Where have you been?" his dad asked when David unlocked the door and let himself in. "Your mom's had Kimberly up and dressed for the trip for nearly two hours! We tried to call you but your phone kept going to voicemail, and now our power is out. They must be working on the lines or something."

"My phone was dead and I didn't have my charger. Josh forgot to wake me up. I'd better use the house phone to call April. Her car died just down the street, and I think it's the battery. I'm gonna be even later than I thought getting back."

David gave his little girl a kiss and apologized to his mom when he went into the kitchen to use the wall phone. He couldn't even charge his cell phone now that the power was out, but after he called her he would walk back to April's car and get her 12-volt charger and plug it into his dad's car. He couldn't remember the last time he'd started a day with so

ENTER THE DARKNESS

many little aggravations, and picking up the receiver to the landline, he discovered yet another one.

"Hey, what's wrong with this phone? I'm not getting a dial tone," he said, turning to his mother.

"I don't know. It was working earlier. I used it several times already trying to reach you on your cell. Is it because the power is out?"

"That shouldn't have anything to do with it," his dad said, walking in on the conversation. "Did you try hanging up and picking it up again?"

"Several times. It's stone dead. There's just nothing."

"Well, I guess I won't be using it to call the power company to report the outage then. Maybe they'll be through with whatever they're doing and get it turned back on soon."

"I hope so. Hey dad, do you mind pulling your car down there where April's went dead to see if we can jump it off? You've got cables right?"

"Of course. I'll get my key. It's probably just a bad battery."

David followed his dad out to the garage and waited while he got in to start the car. If April's car needed a new battery, he was going to have to ask him for a loan, because he had less than forty bucks in his wallet and he knew a battery would be at least twice that. But while he stood there waiting, wondering what was taking him so long, his dad stepped back out of the car and shook his head.

"Mine's dead too, apparently. That doesn't make much sense because I just drove it to the store yesterday. I'll figure out what's wrong with it after we get April's car jumped though. I know you're in a hurry. Run in and ask your mom for the keys to the Infinity. We'll use it to jump off April's and then I'll see if I can jump mine off too."

Mitch came back with the keys and both of them were dumbfound to discover that his mom's car wouldn't start either. Just like April's Honda and his Dad's Chevrolet, her Infinity seemed to have an electrical problem, with the symptoms of a dead battery. Now David was really stuck, and he couldn't tell April anything. She was going to be worried about Kimberly and so mad at him their relationship might not survive it. But what was he supposed to do about it? It wasn't like it was his fault or anything.

His dad suggested they go talk to the neighbor and see if he knew what was going on. Mr. Bryant next door told them his landline was out too, along with everything else in his house. He had a cell phone that wouldn't come back on, and when David's dad told him about their cars he went back inside and got the key to his Dodge truck and tried it to no avail.

"Now why in the world won't my truck crank? This hasn't got anything to do with the power grid."

"There's got to be some explanation for all this," David's dad said. "I think I'll walk over to the donut shop on Hardy

ENTER THE DARKNESS

Street and get a cup of coffee. Maybe someone there will know what's going on."

David didn't really want to walk that far—it was like seven or eight blocks to Hardy Street, but his head was throbbing from the hangover and he needed coffee and something to eat. There was no use standing there staring at all these vehicles that wouldn't start because none of them knew what to do about it.

When they got to the little café they were disappointed to find it closed for business. The doors were open but the lights were out and the employees were unable to serve them because their cash registers were inoperable. Looking up and down the street, David and his dad saw that it was apparently the same at every business they could see. And the strangest thing by far was that the busy four-lane throughway was full of stalled cars and trucks, most of them with their hoods raised. It was like someone had flipped a switch and turned them all off at once, the same as April's Honda. David had never seen anything like it, and neither had his dad. No one they asked seem to know what to make of it either, so they turned around and headed back home. The only thing their excursion accomplished was that David's hangover was nearly gone by the time they got back, cured by all the walking.

"So now what?" David asked, as he and his father stopped at April's car to get the phone charger out before heading to the house.

"I think you're wasting your time with that. Any of these cars probably have enough juice left in the battery to power that charger, but after what we've seen, I don't think a charge is going to help that cell phone. Whatever did this fried your phone along with everything else."

"I can try it at least. What else am I going to do? I've got to call April or she's going to start freaking out, worrying about Kimberly."

"I'm sure, but I don't know how you're going to call her, son. At least the car stopped while you were close to the house. It could have happened when you were on the highway in the middle of nowhere with my granddaughter, so we should be glad of that. I'm sure we'll find out something soon from the city officials or the police to advise us as to what's going on. You'll just have to sit tight and be patient until then. April will be okay, worried or not."

"Maybe, but she may not ever want to see me again, either."

"I can't help you with that, son. The two of you need to work out your differences though. You've got a daughter to think about, you know. It's not like you two are just dating. Your mom and I were hoping the two of you would be married by now."

David didn't reply. His dad didn't really know the full extent of it and there was no use trying to explain. David never planned to be a father at such a young age, if ever. But

ENTER THE DARKNESS

when Kimberly came along, he was a proud daddy, despite the problems he and April had from time to time. He thought he was doing the best he could, but money was tight and everything but his paycheck was going up. April was taking night classes and working too, and David had to spend most of his free time after work taking care of Kimberly while she was gone. Most of the time he didn't mind it, but it seemed he never got to have fun any more. That's why he'd taken advantage of the evening before to get drunk with Josh. It was the first time in a while, but then this had to happen today and it was bound to cause him a world of grief when he and Kimberly finally did make it home. He stopped in the carport to plug the dead iPhone into the cigarette lighter outlet of his dad's car, whether it would do any good or not. The little red LED indicator on the car charger came on, so at least that was working, but the phone did nothing. He left it where it was on the seat and went inside.

Six

"I'VE GOT TO START heading home," Mitch told Mr. Greenfield as they stood there talking where they'd first met beside their stalled vehicles. "My thirteen-year-old sister is going to need me. She's not going to know what to do. I'm sure school will be dismissed today, but I was supposed to pick her up after classes."

Mitch explained that Lisa had stayed overnight with her best friend, who lived with her mom and older brother near the school they all attended. At this hour she should be in her first class, but if the power was off there too as Mitch was sure it was, she wouldn't be able to stay at the school. With him gone and no way for her to call their mom and dad, Lisa wouldn't know what to do. Her only reasonable option was to go back home with Stacy and Jason until Mitch could get there.

"She spent the night there because I had to leave so early to get Mom and Dad to the airport on time. They were flying to Denver for a funeral tomorrow. It was my mom's best friend and college roommate that died. They were supposed

ENTER THE DARKNESS

to be back on Friday. Lisa and I were going to stay at the house after I got home today and we would have been fine, but this changes everything now."

"How are you going to get back? From what you said, your family's place is a long way from here. It took you two hours to drive to the airport from there?"

"Almost. We allowed a little extra, but yeah, it's a little over a hundred miles. To answer your question though, I'll walk. What else can I do?" Mitch asked as he unlocked his truck and began rummaging around behind the seats for something.

"*Walk? More than hundred miles!* Do you know how long that'll take you? It would take me a week to walk a hundred miles!"

"I don't mind walking Mr. Greenfield. It sounds like a long way, but it won't take that long. If what we're guessing about that solar flare is true, they aren't going to get the power back on today, or tomorrow, or this week, or the next. Who knows when they will? I'm a fast walker and I'm in good shape, so I won't need to stop much. I reckon it won't take me more than about three long days to get there… maybe part of a forth."

"But what are you going to do when it gets dark? What are you going to do about food and water? You know, you could come over to my house if you want to wait and see what happens. Deborah, my wife, won't mind. We've got a generator, and other emergency stuff we keep in storage for hurricane season. Things shouldn't be too bad for a few days anyway. Maybe by then this will get resolved."

"I appreciate it, but I can't just sit here and wait. I'd feel cooped up anyway surrounded by all this concrete. No offense if it's your thing, Mr. Greenfield, but I can't stand being in a city even for a little while, and like I said, my little sister's gonna need me. The sooner I get started, the sooner I'll get there."

Mitch was sorting through his things in the truck as he talked and making a small pile on the passenger's seat of what he would take with him. When he was done, his school backpack was bulging at the seams; stuffed with his camouflage hunting clothing he'd planned to change into on the way home. He slung the backpack over his shoulder and unfastened his belt to put on a big hunting knife he took out of the truck next. Mitch then reached behind the seat one more time and pulled out a longbow and a leather quiver full of arrows.

"Good heavens, Mitch! What are you going to do with all that stuff?"

"Well, I'm not about to leave it here in my truck for somebody to break in and steal. This is my favorite hunting bow, and there's just about nothing I would take for it. And there's nothing I'd rather do than hunt, Mr. Greenfield. You asked what I would do about food. I figure it might come in

ENTER THE DARKNESS

handy for that along the way. I just wish I hadn't left my .357 Magnum at home like an idiot. If I were closer to home, it would be under the seat where it stays when I drive anywhere. But coming down here, crossing the state line into Louisiana and all, Dad said I'd better leave it at home since I'm not old enough to get my concealed carry permit. He said there was no telling what some of these New Orleans city cops would do if they caught an underage Mississippi boy carrying a firearm without a permit. And I won't be able to get one until I'm 21."

"Well, aren't you worried about the police seeing you walking down the street with a bow and arrows? They look like weapons to me."

"And they are too, you can be sure of that, Mr. Greenfield. But I won't be waving it around and I'll keep it unstrung for now, so they'll probably just think my bow is a walking stick from a distance. I figure the cops will have more to worry about than one kid taking a walk out of town along the highway. Anyway, I'd rather risk losing it to confiscation than to leave it here and *know* it will be gone before I ever get back to get the truck."

"I don't know, Mitch. I hate that you've apparently got a bad impression of the city. The people here are some of the friendliest I've ever been around. Sure, there's crime, but I think the police will keep things under control until this situation gets resolved."

"Well, you said you weren't here right after Katrina hit, but we were close enough to New Orleans and the coast even up there in the country to see the bad side of it. And all we heard from down here was how bad things were out of hand with the looting and shooting and that it stayed that way for a long time. It took the National Guard and regular soldiers too to stop all that craziness. How do you figure this is going to be any different? People start freaking out just because the lights are out, and now they can't get around either because their cars aren't running. What's going to happen when the stores all run out of food? I don't know about you, but I don't want to find out. You ought to consider getting out yourself, Mr. Greenfield. You and your wife are both welcome to come with me if you can walk that far. We've got plenty of room up there at the farm. One thing about it, lights or no lights, we won't be going hungry. We've got 600 acres of prime river bottom woods. There's so many deer you can't walk a hundred yards without seeing one, and besides that, Dad has cattle on the farm too."

"That sounds like quite the place, Mitch, but Deb would never agree to leave our home to go someplace remote like that. And even if she would agree, we would just slow you down. I can't imagine walking that far really; I'm not looking forward to walking just the four or five miles back to the house, but I guess there's no use hanging around here any longer. Look, why don't you at least walk back there with me

ENTER THE DARKNESS

before you leave? It's not really out of your way, because I can tell you a shortcut to get back to the expressway from the house. We'll load you up with some snack foods and bottled water for your trip, and you can fill up on a hot meal before you set out. What do you say?"

Mitch thought about it for a moment and decided that would probably be the smart thing to do. He didn't have food or water, and he was facing a long trek just to get out of the concrete jungle that was New Orleans and the North Shore cities across the bridge. He had a long way to go before he could even begin to consider hunting along the way.

"Okay. If you're sure you can spare it, I could use a bit of food and water to get started."

"Of course we can. Deb will be glad to fix you up. If I were you, I'd get some rest first too. It's going to get really hot today. You can nap at our house and leave late in the afternoon or early evening if you like. I think it may be smarter walking out of the city at night. You'll have less chance of being seen or hassled that way."

Mitch figured Mr. Greenfield was probably right about that too. As much as he hated to delay getting started, he knew he could make it up by walking all night. Mitch liked walking at night anyway and did it frequently on the farm, sometimes even wandering the national forest lands beyond their property in the dark. He would go with Mr. Greenfield, and then when he left, he was sure he would be able to make it to the North Shore before stopping again.

"I was going to play hooky today," Mitch explained after they set out for Mr. Greenfield's house and the older man asked him why he had the bow and arrows and the hunting clothes in the truck to begin with. "Dad was okay with it, since I was missing my morning classes anyway. I was going to do a little wild hog hunting."

"Really? Is it hunting season now? I thought that was over this time of year."

"It's always hog season back home. Those things aren't native here and they tear up the land and cause all kinds of problems. Besides, my dad's the game warden and if he says it okay, then I don't have to worry about it."

"Game warden, huh? That sounds like an interesting job. I'll bet it's dangerous too though, isn't it?"

"It can be. Dad has his share of run-ins with outlaws and poachers. His department sometimes gets involved in drug cases too, especially when its smugglers or growers operating out in the boonies. But he's good at what he does. Most people around there have heard about his reputation and know better than to push their luck in Stone County."

"Well, I sure hope he and your mom are safe in Houston. It sounds like he's the kind of man that'll be needed back there around home if this situation lasts as long as I'm afraid it might."

"If that plane landed he'll make it home. I have no doubt

ENTER THE DARKNESS

of that. If anybody could do it, my dad could, and he'll take care of my mom too. But it's a long way from Houston without a ride, so I won't be looking for him anytime soon."

Seven

APRIL WAS GROWING MORE anxious by the minute as she began to think that David not getting back on time with Kimberly was somehow connected to the weirdness going on in the city. If she could just find someone with a working phone, she would call him, or if she couldn't reach him, she'd call his parents. Getting to work had suddenly lost its urgency in light of a situation that could be a lot more serious than she'd assumed. Her walk around just one block of the neighborhood was enough to confirm her fears. *No one* she talked to had a working cell phone, and those who'd tried to start their cars discovered they had the same problem as Jennifer. The only exception was a man who had an old diesel-powered Volvo from the early 80's.

"Yes, it still runs just fine," he told her, when she joined the small group of people from the neighborhood who'd walked over to his driveway when they saw that he had a running car. "I don't think it's because of the diesel. I think it's just because it doesn't have the computer the newer cars all have. Whatever caused this power outage had to be some

ENTER THE DARKNESS

kind of atmospheric electrical surge. Nothing else could explain the damaged cell phones and other devices. It must have been widespread enough to take out the telephone company's equipment as well, since the landlines are down too."

"I've never heard of anything like that," April said.

"I don't know that it's ever happened before, but I think it might have been an electromagnetic pulse; sometimes called an 'EMP'."

"What could cause it though? There wasn't a storm or anything," another man asked.

"Not one that we could see, anyway. They say solar activity can cause it. Or a nuclear weapon detonated high above the ground, in the atmosphere. But I doubt it was deliberate. It's not something the terrorists could pull off and the countries that are capable probably wouldn't risk the retaliation they know would follow."

"So what can we do," the same man asked. "How long will it take them to get everything back online?"

"It's not a matter of just getting the city back online. If it was powerful enough to fry even the electronic modules in vehicles, it must have been powerful enough to devastate a vast area. If so, the grid will be down across the whole region, and maybe even the whole country. There won't be enough parts and components to replace a fraction of what's been damaged. It will all have to be rebuilt from scratch. And that's just the power grid. The same thing applies to all communication systems and transportation networks. I doubt any aircraft are flying, especially not commercial. If what I think happened is really true, it's going to be a nightmare beyond anything we've ever seen. It'll be a catastrophic event."

April felt a wave of panic sweep over her as she heard this man's theories. If what he said was true, then how was David supposed to get here at all? What if he hadn't actually overslept? What if he was already on the way and driving when this electromagnetic pulse thing or whatever it was hit? If so, her little Kimberly could be out there on the road somewhere, stranded with David, who would have no way of getting her home. She tried to push that image out of her mind. Surely it wasn't as bad as this man said. Surely the grid couldn't be down as far away as Hattiesburg. For once, she hoped that the worst she'd assumed about David was true; that he'd gone out partying with friends the night before and simply overslept this morning. Because if that were the case and things really were the same there in Hattiesburg as they were here in New Orleans, at least Kimberly would be safe at her grandparent's house. They would look after her until she could find a way to get there, and she *would* if David didn't show up with her soon.

She walked back to her apartment, stopping to tell Jennifer across the street what she'd heard and then Mrs.

ENTER THE DARKNESS

Landry next door before going back inside. She had to calm herself down but she still wanted her morning coffee too, although she knew the caffeine probably wouldn't help her nerves. It didn't matter anyway, because she had no way to make any. Even the stove in the apartment was electric. She settled instead for one of the Cokes David kept in the fridge, even though she hated soft drinks and would never drink one under normal circumstances.

Opening the door to get it out, she realized the refrigerator wasn't going to stay cold for long, and everything in it would be ruined soon. There was enough food in there to last a few days though, and there were some nonperishable canned and packaged goods in the cabinets. That was a good thing, since she had no way to get to a store, but food wasn't really on her mind just yet anyway. Opening the Coke, she walked out the side door to the attached carport on their side of the duplex and looked at David's old Mustang. The man with the Volvo had said that older vehicles wouldn't have been affected by the electrical surge. He said they didn't have the computer box thingys or whatever they were under the hood and that they should start and run just the same as always.

This got her thinking, because David's Mustang was a 1969 model—much older than that Volvo she'd just seen running. The problem though, was that David's car was an unreliable piece of junk. At least that was her impression of it. She couldn't count the times he'd called her from somewhere in the city to come pick him up because it had broken down and left him stranded. He spent way more of his meager paycheck on it than she thought was reasonable, especially for a man with a daughter. April and David had fought about that car numerous times, and had almost broken up because of it. The latest incident resulted in him paying to have it towed home, where he'd pushed it under the side carport and it had been sitting for weeks. April had been giving him rides when she could and occasionally letting him use her car when she was feeling especially benevolent towards him.

One of his friends with more mechanical knowledge than he had told David he needed to rebuild the carburetor, and he'd bought the parts to do it and removed it, but hadn't started taking it apart yet. April looked at the tools scattered on an old table next to the car and reached in the open window and took out the box that contained the rebuild kit. She didn't know much about working on cars, but she'd helped her dad change the oil in his and she had at least a passing familiarity with basic hand tools, such as wrenches and screwdrivers. Opening the box of parts, she saw that there was an exploded diagram sheet that showed where all the bits and pieces went, and she began to think that if David could figure it out, she probably could too. But that was a last resort that could wait a bit for now, because she still held out

ENTER THE DARKNESS

hope that he would somehow get there with Kimberly.

* * *

It took an hour and a half for Mitch and Mr. Greenfield to walk to his house near the Lakeshore. The older man wasn't in great shape so Mitch let him set the pace for the 5-mile journey, doing his best to remain patient as he tagged along. He would make up for lost time by traveling hard through the night, and the promised food that awaited him at Mr. Greenfield's house would make that possible. He thought the man was making a mistake by choosing to stay there in the city with his wife, but Mitch had invited him to come to the farm and that was all he could really do. He understood the instinct to stay at home in familiar surroundings in a time of crisis, but the more he thought about this situation, the more he realized an urban area like this was the wrong place to be. He didn't know exactly what the population of New Orleans was, but it was the biggest city in the region between Atlanta and Houston. No matter the number, he knew there were a *lot* of people in the Big Easy and they were going to be desperate if this situation was really as serious as he now thought it was. To Mitch's way of thinking, the only hope of avoiding trouble was to be in a place where people were few and far between, and the Henley farm fit that description perfectly.

He'd already seen the beginnings of panic within the first few minutes of being stranded back at that intersection. The plane crashes started it, and now as they walked they saw more and more frantic people hurrying in all directions along the streets. Stalled cars and trucks were everywhere, but there were a few vehicles still running too, weaving their way among the rest blocking the lanes. Without exception, those that were running were older models; some of them work trucks and light delivery trucks, beater cars and a surprising number of motorcycles, mostly older Harley Davidsons with loud pipes that could be heard long before they were close.

"That proves what the scientists were saying," Mitch said, as he and Mr. Greenfield discussed this.

"Yes, I'd say so. The only vehicles moving appear to be from the 80's or older."

"It's too bad I wasn't in my Grandpa's old truck. I know it wasn't affected. It's a 1961 Ford with a straight 6-cylinder and 3-speed on the column shift. I could drive right out of here if we'd come in that today instead of Dad's new truck."

"That just goes to show you that newer isn't always better, is it?"

"Nope. But most people think it is. I wonder though, if trying to drive out of here wouldn't be even risker than walking though."

"How so?"

"Well, look how many other people are stuck. What if

someone really desperate decided they'd rather ride than walk? People might start carjacking pretty soon."

"Maybe, but again, Mitch, I think you give the bad element too much credit. Sure, we have our share, but most people are going to come together and try and help each other out, rather than steal from them."

"I hope you're right, Mr. Greenfield. I really do. I'm just thinking of the possible scenarios, that's all. It's a habit I have, probably from spending so much time alone in the woods, hunting."

"I've never hunted, but I imagine the spending time alone part is nice. That's something I don't get much of."

"I imagine not, living here. How could you?"

"We used to have a boat a few years ago. Deborah and I would go sailing on the Pontchartrain to watch the sunset after work and sometimes we'd spend the whole day out there on Sundays. It was a nice escape to peace and quiet once in a while."

"Too bad you don't still have it. I imagine a boat could be a good option for getting out of here when things get worse."

"Maybe. But where would we go? If the damage is really widespread, it's going to be the same everywhere. We'll be as well off here as anywhere else, I think."

Mitch disagreed, but he decided to drop the subject. He had more to worry about than trying to convince a stranger of what he should do. His thoughts wandered back to his parents, and he hoped and prayed they were safely on the ground because no matter how chaotic things might get in a city the size of Houston they would have a chance as long as their plane had landed in time. Mitch had complete faith in his father's abilities to get the two of them home, but he also knew it would take some time. While they were gone, he was going to have to look after Lisa as well as take care of the house and the farm. He figured he would have plenty of time to do so, because he didn't see any way that the school could continue to operate. People were going to have to take care of themselves, and out in the country where he was from, most knew how. But that didn't mean it was going to be easy. Mitch knew what it was like living without power for a few days, but this time it was going to be much longer and the disruption of communications and transportation would make it exponentially harder.

Eight

APRIL SPENT MUCH OF the day pacing the floor when she was inside and walking out to the street to talk to anyone she saw passing by to see if they knew anything. No one had any real news beyond the immediate vicinity. As the day wore on, more people were moving about though, and she saw far more bicycles on the street than usual. A bicycle made a lot of sense in this situation, but April didn't have one and neither did David. Some of the people she saw riding by on them had obviously ridden to the grocery stores, as they were carrying bags tied to their handlebars and anywhere else they could put them. She talked to one man whose bike was so heavily loaded that he was pushing it along, and his story was not encouraging.

"People are going nuts! It's worse than when a hurricane is coming. They're cleaning out the stores—at least all the ones that are open. Those that are can only take cash, because they have no way to verify credit cards or checks. But even so, there are lines out the doors."

"I'm glad I don't need anything today then," April said.

ENTER THE DARKNESS

"You'd better be thinking about a lot longer than today, young lady. They're saying everything will be gone by tomorrow, if it's not already. And a lot of people are saying there won't be anyone coming to restock because the trucks aren't running. Think about it! It's like this *everywhere!*"

April didn't want to think about it. It was a nightmare too frightening to contemplate. All she wanted to think about was getting her Kimberly back in her arms. Her baby was only a little over a year old. She needed her mother and that was all there was to it.

When the afternoon faded away into evening and finally full darkness, April found herself in a blacked-out New Orleans that was darker than she could have ever imagined a modern city could be. If the darkness itself weren't strange enough, the quiet in the absence of machinery was surreal—especially at night when sound carried so much farther. The predominate sounds she heard now were human voices—the chatter of conversation, laughter and argument. There were screams and curses, crying children, and barking dogs, but no roar from the nearby interstate, or from trains on the tracks or airplanes overhead. And then much later, sometime after midnight by her best guess, the loudest sounds that reached her ears through the walls of the old wood frame house were gunshots. It wasn't the first time she'd heard shots fired late at night from her apartment, but incidents like that were few and far between in her relatively safe neighborhood. She didn't know what the shooting was about, but someone fired at least half a dozen rounds in rapid succession from what sounded like a semiautomatic rifle.

The big difference this time and the other times she'd heard gunfire in the city was that the shots were not followed by the sounds of police sirens. Some of the people she had talked to earlier mentioned this, saying that the police were just as helpless as everyone else with their cruisers inoperable and their communication networks down. Without a dispatcher to take calls and coordinate a response, how could they effectively do anything? Thinking of this made April wish she had a gun of her own, but she didn't and neither did David. Her father had taught her how to shoot both rifles and pistols before he'd died, and he had owned several nice weapons that he'd left to her mom, but she had sold them all without telling April. It had infuriated her when she found out, but then her mom had her accident and April forgot her anger. Losing both of her parents before she was even eighteen years old had been devastating, but she'd gotten through it when Kimberly came along and gave her a new reason to live.

David knew nothing of firearms anyway and had little interest in them, and money had been tight as long as she'd been with him, so purchasing a handgun or shotgun for home defense had been pushed far down the list of priorities. April regretted that unfortunate decision now. She could easily see

ENTER THE DARKNESS

how things could get really out of hand if help from outside didn't arrive soon. It had been horrible here during Hurricane Katrina, but thankfully, she'd only seen that on the news because at the time both of her parents were still alive and she was living with them in Dallas. She felt a little safer knowing she at least had the martial arts skills her father had taught her, including not only empty hand techniques but knife and stick methods as well. The big Spyderco folding knife she kept clipped in the back pocket of her jeans was a comfort, but she knew she'd feel better with a pistol to go with it.

Even if she hadn't heard the gunshots, April couldn't have slept that first night after the blackout. She paced the floor and looked outside, hoping for some slim chance that she would see David pulling into the driveway with Kimberly. It didn't happen though and daylight finally came, finding April utterly exhausted but still too upset to get any rest. She waited until there was more activity in the neighborhood, and then went back out to the street. It had been about 24 hours now, and nothing had changed, other than the fact that more people were out walking and riding places on bicycles. The cars that wouldn't start yesterday still sat immobile today.

"I heard the shooting too," Jennifer said, when April crossed the street to talk to her after seeing her step outside. "I wondered what it was. I hope no one was hurt."

"Yeah me too, but I'm afraid people will be. I've got to

get out of here. I've got to get to my daughter. I don't think her father is going to be able to get back here."

April told Jennifer about the old Mustang and the repairs it needed. Jennifer had seen it sitting there under the carport, broken down and useless more often than not. All she could do for April was wish her luck. She didn't have a clue about things mechanical. April left her house to walk down and see the man who had the running Volvo. She thought that maybe if he kept such an old vehicle well maintained and running, he might be able to help her, or at least offer some advice. But when she got there, she wasn't completely surprised to see that the old sedan was gone. Evidently, the owner and his wife had decided to get out of town while they still could. She wondered where to, but it didn't really matter. They were gone and she hoped they made it somewhere safe. And she was on her own to figure out how to do the same.

* * *

Mr. Greenfield's house was an expensive-looking older home that appeared to be immaculately maintained. All the houses along his street were upscale, the front lawns shaded by grand old Live oak trees and a variety of exotic palms and subtropical plants. A shiny BMW sports car was parked in the circular brick drive in front of the house, and Mr. Greenfield breathed a sigh of relief at the sight of the car.

ENTER THE DARKNESS

"I didn't think she would be out and about before this pulse or whatever it was happened, but I was still worried. She was getting ready to go run some errands when I left for work."

When they went inside and Mitch was introduced to Deborah Greenfield, she told them she had gone out to try and start her car right after the power went out.

"At least we still have one car at home in case there's a way to get parts for it later. Mine is sitting in the middle of the road right behind this young man's pickup truck."

Mr. Greenfield explained to his wife what Mitch intended to do, and she readily agreed that they would help him prepare and load him down with all the food he could carry.

"I told him we'd feed him well before he left too. I'm going to go out back and clean off the grill. We can have those steaks you bought yesterday and maybe wrap up some potatoes and onions in foil to go with them."

Mr. Greenfield made good on his promise and Mitch stuffed himself until he was full. After eating he stretched out in a comfortable hammock beside the swimming pool and soon dozed off into a deep sleep. When he awoke he knew from the angle of the sun that it was already late afternoon, and his watch confirmed that it was after 4:30. He hadn't expected to sleep so long, but then again, he had gotten up hours earlier than usual so that he and his parents could leave the Henley farm before 4 a.m. The long nap and the filling meal would do him good, and he was ready to get moving on his journey. But when he walked back to the patio in the courtyard between the house and pool, he found that the Greenfields had prepared even more food and were insistent that he eat again before leaving.

"We had plenty of shrimp in the freezer that needs to be eaten," Mr. Greenfield explained as he lifted the lid off a huge pot of creole gumbo he had boiling over a propane cooker. Mitch noticed the lights on inside the house as well, and the low hum of a diesel generator running somewhere nearby. "I told you we were set up to deal with hurricanes. We'll be quite comfortable and well-fed here for at least a couple of weeks."

The gumbo was irresistible and Mitch knew it wouldn't matter if he waited another hour to get started. He ate two bowlfuls and washed it down with sweet iced tea, finishing just about the time the sun was going down. Deborah Greenfield had laid out a huge assortment of snack foods, including energy bars and several MREs and six packs of bottled water for Mitch's journey. It was far more than he could carry, but he stuffed two of the MREs, a few high protein energy bars and a half dozen of the water bottles into his small backpack. There was just enough room in it after he removed the hunting coveralls and lashed them to the outside. He would put them on as soon as he was out of the city.

ENTER THE DARKNESS

Mr. Greenfield dug up a state map of Louisiana for Mitch before he left, and the two of them studied it until Mitch had a pretty good idea of the best route to take and the approximate distances involved. The options for leaving the city were rather limited because of Lake Pontchartrain, but the most direct route was the same one he had driven in on—the Interstate 10 Twin Span Bridge. This bridge was much shorter than the 25-mile-long Causeway and would take him to Slidell on the North Shore. Once across, he would have to make his way through that smaller city either along the interstate, which turned into Interstate 59 going northeast, or the older parallel route of Highway 11. There was little choice for crossing the Pearl River and the surrounding expanse of Honey Island Swamp other than the I-59 Bridge, but after that he'd be over the state line and into Mississippi. Once there, Mitch knew he could leave the interstate again and follow secondary roads to his destination. It appeared to be about 40 miles to the state line where he would feel home free. He was going to have to pace himself because he would still have more than 60 miles to go after that to reach the Henley farm and home. That meant he'd have to find a place to bivouac tomorrow while he was still in Louisiana. It would be a hard push, but he hoped to at least get to the North Shore before doing so.

Nine

AFTER HEARING MR. SMITH'S theory as to what had happened that morning, Lisa and Stacy decided they'd better find Jason and tell him. There was no use hanging around the school because classes were going to be postponed indefinitely if what the science teacher said was true.

"She sometimes has to stay over at the end of her shift if there's a lot going on," Stacy said, as they wondered about her mother. "I hope that's the reason she was late."

"I hope so too. At least if she's stuck at the hospital where she works she'll be safe."

"Yeah, but if what Mr. Smith said was true, then how will she get home at all? He said it wouldn't be easy to get everybody's car fixed because so many of them are going to need new parts. That would be bad enough, but I can't even call her to see if she's okay or to tell her we are. This is pretty crazy, Lisa. I know your mom and dad are probably stuck somewhere and they're going to be worried too."

"They are, and I'm worried about them and Mitch too. But I don't know what I can do. I guess we'll just have to wait

ENTER THE DARKNESS

and see."

When they found Jason he was with a group of high school boys that were crowded around Rusty Sinclair's 1971 Chevy Nova. Lisa heard the engine rumbling as they walked up. The hood was up and Lisa knew Rusty was showing off the big V-8 engine that was his pride and joy. Rusty had restored the old car with the help of his father, and the way he drove it everyone at the school was expecting him to total it out sooner or later. Now he was gloating over the fact that it was still running perfectly, when all of the newer cars and pickups the other students drove were not.

"Mr. Smith said this was caused by a solar flare," Stacy said to Jason when he told them that for some reason, it seemed that older vehicles weren't affected.

"He said it created some kind of pulse that fried sensitive electronics, like cell phones and the computers that control the power grid and even car engines," Lisa added. "He was talking to the principal when we asked him. They are going to be closing down the school and the teachers are going to tell everyone to go home until further notice."

"We might as well leave now then," Jason said. "What about Mom, though? How will she get back from Hattiesburg?"

Lisa was starting at Rusty's Nova when a thought suddenly occurred to her. "Hey, we've got my Grandpa's old truck out at the farm! It's even older than Rusty's car, so it wouldn't have been damaged. If we could get it, we could drive to Hattiesburg and pick up your mom!"

"Hey, you're probably right," Jason said. "The only problem with that idea is that it's a long way to your farm and we don't have a ride."

"Maybe Rusty would drive us," Stacy said.

Rusty couldn't hear any of this conversation because he was still sitting in the driver's seat of his car, revving the engine and talking to the other boys crowded around him. Lisa doubted he would be interested in driving them all the way to the Henley farm because Rusty Sinclair had a reputation for doing what Rusty wanted and the heck with anyone else. Jason said the same thing, and it wasn't like he was one of Rusty's friends anyway. Rusty was the quarterback of the varsity football team, and like Mitch, Jason didn't even play high school sports. Neither of them were going to be winning any high school popularity contests, and neither cared. Mitch was into the woods and Jason dug his guitar.

"It won't even do any good to ask him," he told his little sister. "Come on. Let's just all walk back to the house and think about this a bit. Maybe mom will find a way to get there. I think we ought to give her a little time. What if we're gone and she comes home and can't find us? She won't have any way to call us."

"We could leave her a note," Stacy said.

"Yeah, and we will if we leave, but let's wait and see for a

ENTER THE DARKNESS

bit."

"That's probably a good idea," Lisa agreed. "Mitch might find a way to get here too, and if he does, he's going to come to the school or to your house first, looking for me."

When they got there, Stacy's mom wasn't back, not that any of them had really expected her to be.

"What are we going to do all day?" Stacy wondered. "It's going to be boring without TV."

"At least we won't have to listen to Jason's guitar playing," Lisa said. Jason had already gone to his room. He probably already had his guitar out, but if he did, they couldn't hear it without the amplifier. "We can play a game or something."

"Yeah, I guess. I'm just worried about Mom though. I wish I knew for sure that she was still at the hospital."

"I know. I'm worried about my mom and dad too, and my brother. Maybe we just need to stop thinking about it so much though. We can't do anything about it right now. If she's not back by tomorrow we can go get the old truck somehow and go look for her. I'm sure she'll be fine until then."

* * *

Little Kimberly was whining and restless and no doubt wanting her mommy when David Greene went back inside his parents' house. He had no idea how he was going to get his little girl back home, or even let her mother know that the two of them were okay. He wondered too if he was going to lose his job over this. He had no way to contact his supervisor and he'd already been warned about being late more than once. He had been on thin ice there for at least a couple of months and this was going to make it worse. David hated his current job as much as he'd hated every job he'd ever had, but he didn't have many choices and at least he got some overtime most weeks. He needed it because it was so expensive living with April in New Orleans. The rent was the worst part, but there were a lot of things Kimberly needed too and even though April made as much as he did, David had very little left for himself from his meager paychecks. Things had certainly been easier when he still lived in Hattiesburg, hanging out with Josh and his other buddies and drinking beer almost every night. But then he'd met April by chance and his life had changed forever. After spending time with her, nothing he was doing before seemed important, at least in the beginning. After a few weeks of this, David found himself looking for a job in New Orleans. They hadn't planned on Kimberly, but once they knew she was coming they were determined to stay together. David had done his best in the beginning, he really had, but he knew he was becoming a disappointment to April. He knew she worked harder than he did and didn't seem to mind it, yet he felt cheated out of his youth and not ready for so much

ENTER THE DARKNESS

responsibility and a life with little to look forward to but going to work every day.

He still dreamed of restoring the classic Mustang his uncle had given him before he graduated high school, but there was never any extra money to put into it. He couldn't even keep it running most of the time; much less afford things like the new upholstery and paint job it needed to be really cool. David knew he needed to figure out a way to get ahead, but so far the answer as to how to do that had eluded him. April was angry with him about as often as not, and the friction was beginning to take its toll.

Thinking about all this, David realized that in a way he was relieved that he couldn't go home. Maybe a forced break away from April for a few days was what they both needed. It would be better if it were just him stranded here while Kimberly was with her, but he had his mom and dad to help him with the child, so that wasn't going to be too big of a deal. Josh's apartment wasn't exactly close, but it was within walking distance if he wanted to go hang out and drink a beer. No one could blame him if he did, because none of this was really his fault. April would in fact be thankful that he'd overslept this morning when she found out, because if he hadn't, he and Kimberly might be stuck on the side of Interstate 59 somewhere between Hattiesburg and New Orleans. That would be a real problem, he realized, so no matter what April thought about it, getting drunk last night was the best decision he'd made in a while.

David's father was deep in thought while his mother took Kimberly to her rocking chair and sat down with her to try and sooth her. David was headed for his old room to lie down and take a nap when his father stopped him.

"Son, I think we'd better get busy. The more I think about this, the more worried I get. You saw all those broken down cars sitting in the middle of Hardy Street. Whatever caused this, it was something really serious, and we don't have any way to find out the full extent of it. I think we need to get down to the nearest grocery store and try and pick up all the food we can before it's too late."

"How are we gonna buy anything, Dad? You heard what they said at the donut shop. Their cash registers aren't working and they can't take plastic or checks."

"I know that, but the grocery store might be willing to take cash. They're going to have a lot of things like meats and produce and dairy that will ruin if they can't get rid of it. I've got some cash on hand. It's worth a try to get what we can before other people get it all, because we don't know how long this situation is going to last."

"Even if you buy things like that, we won't be able to keep them from spoiling either," David's mom said.

"No, but I'm thinking they may sell their non-perishables too. Why wouldn't they? They're going to have to close their doors soon, I'm sure, but the owners will probably be glad to

ENTER THE DARKNESS

make all the money they can before they have to. Especially at the smaller stores."

"How are we supposed to get there?" David asked. "If we just walk, how are we going to bring anything back?"

"That's what I've been thinking about. I've got my riding mower out back in the garden shed. It should crank just fine because all it has is a battery and a simple starter and relay. There's gas in the tank because I just filled it a couple of days ago and I didn't cut the lawn because it rained. I've got that little leaf trailer I bought for it that I can tow behind it, and it will haul a lot of groceries if we fill it up."

"Hmmm. I guess that might work. But two people can't ride on it, so why do you need me?"

"Because I might have a problem, son. The mower may break down on the way there or on the way back, and if we both go, the two of us can carry a few bags of groceries in our hands too. That thing is as slow as walking anyway. If you don't want to walk, you can drive it and I'll walk. We can switch up on the way back."

David saw that there was no way out of this and that his nap wasn't going to happen. He followed his dad out to the garden shed, and just like the old man said, the mower started right up without issue. They hooked up the little trailer and his dad went back inside to get his money. Maybe it would be worth it if they could indeed buy something, but David still had his doubts. He wondered what April was doing right now and figured she was probably going crazy with worry. She would have to know by now that he wasn't going to be able to get home with Kimberly. If she were here with him then he wouldn't have much to worry about. They could just stay at his mom and dad's house until things got fixed. But with April that far away, David didn't know what to do. All he could think of was that maybe they would hear something soon from the power company or other officials and maybe the authorities would get some buses or something running like they did for hurricane evacuations. If they did, maybe he could ride one to New Orleans to get April. Or maybe there would be one she could catch to Hattiesburg. Other than that, he was out of ideas.

Ten

APRIL WENT BACK HOME after her walk around the neighborhood and ate some leftover pizza from the fridge with another one of David's Cokes. Things inside there were barely cool now, and the ice cream and other goods in the freezer were beginning to thaw out and melt. She would eat all of the perishable items she could and save the few cans and packaged items in the cabinets for later—hopefully for her journey to Hattiesburg.

With that thought in mind, she went out to the carport and felt around under the front edge of the Mustang's hood for the latch. When she lifted it up, she saw the place on the top of the engine where the carburetor went, the hole now covered with a greasy rag. David had pointed out the carburetor to her before when he told her he was going to rebuild it, but she'd barely had a passing interest then. Now, she wished she'd paid more attention, but she knew that everything he'd taken off the car had to go back the same way it was before. There was only one way the parts could fit together, and she was determined to figure it out. He had put

ENTER THE DARKNESS

the carburetor in an old cardboard box and laid that on the passenger's side floorboards. April took the entire box and its contents into the kitchen, along with the new, smaller box that contained the rebuild kit. Then she went back out to the carport and collected all the screwdrivers, wrenches and sockets she saw scattered around. If she was going to do this, she wanted to be comfortable, because it was going to take some time. The dining table was perfect for her purpose because it was next to a big window that let in plenty of sunlight during the daytime.

She unfolded the sheet with the diagram again and studied it carefully, and then took out each of the new parts that came with the kit and compared them to what she could see in the illustration. Most of the parts were gaskets and little metal clips and springs. There were a *lot* of them though, and April began to think that maybe this wasn't going to be as easy as she thought. She was going to have to carefully disassemble the carburetor and take careful notes of how everything she took apart went together, and then identify all the old parts the new ones were to replace, and install them one-by-one as she put it all back together. She could only hope that rebuilding the carburetor was all that the car needed to run. She wasn't exactly sure how David's friend came to that conclusion, but she did know that for a long time the car wouldn't run at idle without going dead and then it had gotten to where it wouldn't start at all. He said it was because the inside of the carburetor was gummed up, and that tearing it down and cleaning everything and then putting it back together with the new parts in the rebuild kit would make it as good as new. It was all April had to go on and she knew it was her best hope if she wanted to get to Hattiesburg.

When she began removing screws and taking the carburetor apart, she could see that it was indeed dirty, both inside and out, but then so was most everything else under the hood of the old car. She scribbled notes to herself on a piece of paper as she worked; drawing her own diagrams so she would remember where everything she took off came from. The little parts that would be replaced by new ones in the kit she put aside in one pile, while laying out the bigger pieces that would be reused on the table so she could clean them one-by-one. She had seen David using mineral spirits to soak greasy parts for cleaning when he was doing other repairs on the Mustang, so she went back out to the carport and looked until she found a quart container among his collection of oils and other lubricants and cleaners. She poured some in a shallow bowl and sloshed the parts around, relieved to see that it did indeed loosen the crud and grease caked on them and now on her fingers as well. The soaking plus wiping with paper towels made the parts shiny again and would make them much easier to work with as she reassembled the unit.

ENTER THE DARKNESS

April had no idea how much time passed as she concentrated on her work, but when direct sunlight no longer illuminated the table by the window, she knew it had to be well after noon. She took a break and went outside to see what was going on in the neighborhood. It was quiet on her street, but she could hear shouting several blocks away in the direction of the nearest commercial district, and from somewhere in that area, a dense plume of dark smoke was rising over the tops of the buildings. Just as when she had heard the gunshots during the night, there were no sirens wailing in response to what had to be a building or house fire. April wondered if it was deliberate arson and figured that it probably was. With no firefighters to put it out, whatever was burning would likely be totally destroyed, and April wondered how much more of the city would burn because of all this. Were the looters that were surely stripping grocery stores and other businesses of their goods also setting fires before they left? April knew such things were common in riot conditions, and she figured that rioting was surely already taking place in parts of the city. People had probably already died because of this and April was afraid the number was going to rise rapidly in the coming days. She had to get out before it got so bad that she couldn't. Even if Kimberly and David were here with her, they would have no choice now but to get out. It would be impossible to survive in a place like New Orleans in these conditions. She hoped that Hattiesburg would be different. It was a much smaller city with a far lower population density and a lot less crime in normal times. Things might get bad there, but she couldn't imagine they would ever be as bad as they were surely going to be here.

It tore her apart thinking about what would become of people like Mrs. Landry, next door. The sweet old lady lived alone and didn't drive, but she did have a somewhat younger sister in Slidell who came by at least once a week and brought her groceries and the other things she needed, usually staying all day when she did. April hadn't seen the sister since the lights went out though, so she thought she'd better go next door again and check on Mrs. Landry herself before it got dark again.

* * *

"Are you sure you don't want to wait until morning to get started?" Deborah Greenfield asked Mitch as he folded the map and tucked it into his pack. "You can get a good night's sleep in a comfortable bed and I'll make you a big breakfast."

"No ma'am, I appreciate it, but I'm sure. I want to get going right now and make as much time as I can before morning. I don't plan on stopping until I'm on the other side of that bridge. I can't thank you enough for all the good food and the supplies, though. It will make all the difference for my trip home."

ENTER THE DARKNESS

"We're glad to help. I don't envy your journey, but you're young and strong and I'm sure you'll be fine. We wish you the best of luck."

"And good luck to both of you too. I really hope things don't get too out of hand here, but if they do, y'all better get out of the city somehow—before it's too late. Keep your eyes and ears open."

"We will, Mitch. Don't worry about us. Just do your best to avoid trouble on the road. I know you will," Mr. Greenfield said.

"I'll be fine, I'm not worried about myself. It's my sister I'm concerned about. I think she'll be okay until I get there, but we've got work to do on the farm to prepare for what I imagine is going to be a long wait for my mom and dad."

Mitch shook hands with Mr. Greenfield one last time and then set out down the street to follow the shortcut his new acquaintance had sketched to take him back to the expressway. He heard more generators running in the neighborhood, evidence that the well-to-do residents that lived there were better prepared than most. Even so, Mitch didn't see how they could stay there indefinitely. What was going to happen when the hundreds of thousands of people living throughout the rest of the city ran out of food and everything else they needed to live? They were going to start looking for it wherever they could find it, Mitch knew. They would sweep through here like every other neighborhood and take what was left—if anything was. And Mitch knew there would be nothing Mr. Greenfield or anyone else could do to stop them. But that wasn't his worry. He had expressed his concerns and the Greenfield's had made their choice. All he could do was look out for his own, and right now that was Lisa. He'd agreed to be responsible for her while his parents were away, and no matter how long that turned out to be, he aimed to honor his promise.

Mitch soon came to the expressway and had to walk up a long entrance ramp to reach it. He could have stayed on surface streets until he reached the beginning of the bridge across the lake, but after discussing it with Mr. Greenfield, he decided he'd probably encounter fewer people on the elevated roadway. Those that were using it this first night after the blackout were probably stranded motorists who'd left their disabled vehicles hours earlier and were trying to get home.

Their stalled vehicles were everywhere, sitting in random spots in all three lanes, abandoned with their hoods up and doors locked. Some had been pushed off to the outside of the lanes close to the concrete retaining walls, probably because they were part of a cluster and blocking the path of the few vehicles that were still running. As he walked, the occasional car, truck or motorcycle came weaving through, and as he'd noted before all of the ones still moving were either old or of antiquated design not reliant upon electronic components.

ENTER THE DARKNESS

He passed a few other people here and there traveling on foot like him, most of them looking completely exhausted, as they had undoubtedly already walked for miles from wherever they had started when they were stranded. Most of them paid little attention to Mitch, and he likewise avoided interactions with them because there was simply no need to waste time chatting with strangers he would never see again. He was facing hours of steady hiking to get out of the urban zone and into the countryside where he would feel at ease, and he was determined not to let anyone or anything slow him down. He set a pace that would allow him to make maximum time while staying well below the threshold of getting winded. It was a pace he could maintain through the coming night and beyond as long as he kept his focus and didn't stop. Since he had a full belly and enough water in his backpack to sustain him, he had no need to stop other than for a quick drink every couple of hours.

Mitch figured that most residents of the city would be inclined to stay home, like Mr. and Mrs. Greenfield. People wouldn't realize at first how dire the situation would get, but the more he thought about it, the more convinced he was that life here would be unsustainable. When they did figure it out, Mitch knew there would be a mass exodus of refugees fleeing the city, and the bridges across the lake would become bottlenecks when they did. He planned to be long gone by then though, and that resolve kept him putting one foot in front of the other without pause.

Eleven

IT TOOK A FEW minutes of repetitive knocking, but Mrs. Landry finally came to the door before April gave up.

"The phone line is still out, dear. I'm sorry."

"I know that, Mrs. Landry. It's not going to get fixed anytime soon either. I know your sister usually comes by to check on you and she can't now, so I thought I'd better see if you're okay."

"Julie was supposed to come today, dear, but she didn't show up, so I'm a little upset with her. I suppose she had her reasons, but with the phones out I couldn't call her to ask."

"She's not going to be able to drive here, Mrs. Landry. I'm sure her car was affected just like most vehicles were. The only ones that will run are the old ones, like that Mustang of David's. I'm working on it now, trying to get it running, and when I do, I'm going to Hattiesburg because that's where my baby is. When I leave, you're welcome to ride with me to Slidell. I can take you to Julie's house because it can't be all that far out of my way. The interstate goes right through Slidell on the way to Mississippi."

ENTER THE DARKNESS

"Oh I can't do that, dear. I don't think I can stand to stay at Julie's house; she's got all those cats inside that I'm allergic to, and their litter boxes just smell awful! Besides, I would be in your way. You don't need to worry about me because I've got everything I need right here. I'm not going to go hungry for a long time whether Julie comes or not. I've always kept more in the pantry than I'll ever need. You know how it is, living with hurricanes."

"I do, but this is different, Mrs. Landry. You *are* going to run out of everything eventually and Julie won't be able to get here to help you. Besides that, it's not safe here. I've already heard gunshots and seen smoke from a burning building, and the police can't do anything about it. You really should ride with me to your sister's house. At least you won't be alone there. I imagine that most of the neighbors around here are going to try and leave somehow, even if they have to walk or ride bikes. I've been seeing a lot of bikes out since yesterday."

"Oh I'm far too old for that! I wouldn't attempt it even if I had a bike, especially not in this heat."

"Then ride with me. I'm confident I'll be able to get that old Mustang going, maybe by tonight, but definitely by tomorrow. I'm going to get back to work on it right now while there's still light enough to see. I'll let you know in time for you to get some of your things together before I leave. Please think about it, Mrs. Landry."

April understood the old woman's reluctance, but she

couldn't just leave her here. Taking her would mean she couldn't pack as many of her clothes and other possessions into the Mustang, but she was willing to make that sacrifice if Mrs. Landry would go.

She went back to her kitchen and sat down at the table to figure out the next step in the carburetor rebuild. With all the necessary disassembly completed and the parts that would be reused cleaned and ready to put back together, April hoped to have it finished shortly. It didn't happen though, because she accidentally knocked the container in which she'd put the smallest springs and washers off the table. The light coming into the kitchen window that late in the afternoon was too dim to see well enough to find them all, especially since she heard them bounce all over the room when they hit the floor. Some of them ended up under the refrigerator and some between the cabinets. April was frustrated at her carelessness and was kicking herself for leaving her only flashlight in her car. She went to get the one she'd seen in David's toolbox earlier, but of course it didn't work. The batteries were dead and she couldn't find any spares, not that she'd expected to, knowing how he neglected his stuff.

Not ready to give up, April went back to Mrs. Landry's door to see if she had a flashlight she could borrow. But there was no answer after several rounds of loud knocking, and April figured her neighbor was either in the bathroom and couldn't come to the door, or had already gone to bed. She

ENTER THE DARKNESS

returned to her kitchen and felt around on the floor with her fingers, finding some of the small parts but probably not all of them. She couldn't finish the work anyway until she had enough light again to study the diagram and see what she was doing, so she reluctantly quit for the night. It was going to be frustrating waiting for morning, but there was little else she could do. She paced the floor until she was exhausted, finally lying down in her bed many hours after nightfall. The surreal quiet in the city was punctuated by more distant gunfire, and April tossed and turned as worst case scenarios played over and over in her head—especially thoughts of her little Kimberly with no one to protect her but her foolish and irresponsible father.

* * *

The sun sank below the urban horizon behind him as Mitch made his way east along I-610. From the elevated roadway, he had a good view of the skyline of downtown New Orleans, including the unmistakable shape of the Superdome. In the twilight the tall buildings were dark silhouettes against a gray background, the city completely blacked-out and strangely silent. It was an alien environment to Mitch, regardless of the blackout. He didn't like the feeling of being surrounded by concrete and steel in all directions, including the roadway beneath his feet. What he longed for was the woods, and never had he felt so far out of his comfort zone as he did in that last half hour before darkness enveloped New Orleans.

He was still carrying the longbow unstrung, as he had earlier when walking the city streets in the daylight with Mr. Greenfield. He felt it was best to continue keeping as low a profile as possible, and appearing unarmed was the best way to do that. His quiver of arrows was lashed to the side of his daypack, an extra T-shirt wrapped around the cluster of fletching protruding from the top to hide them from view. Mitch hoped he wouldn't need the bow and arrows to defend himself, but since he was so out of his element and alone in a strange environment at night, he couldn't help but feel a little nervous. At least on the expressway he had long sight lines without trees and other places of concealment near his route, as would be the case on the surface streets. He knew he could string the bow and draw an arrow in less than half a minute if he needed to, but he hoped he wouldn't have to put the bow to use until he hit the woods farther north, where there would be game to hunt along the way.

Thinking of hunting as he walked, Mitch began to realize that his woodsman's skills were about to become of prime importance if the effects he saw here in New Orleans were indeed widespread. Most people were going to suffer greatly in the absence of the easy living that was all they had ever known—a lifestyle made possible only by modern

ENTER THE DARKNESS

technology. But Mitch knew he could live without that stuff because he did it willingly as often as his parents and his school schedule would allow. He'd first taken to hunting and all things outdoors as he tagged along behind his father as a little boy. Doug Henley was a great teacher and far more knowledgeable about such things than most. He'd built a career around his love of hunting and fishing and had earned quite the reputation as a game warden in his home county. But Mitch was even more obsessed with hunting than his dad. He took it several steps further, first by mastering archery so he could hunt like the Indians he read so much about, and then learning to make his own primitive bows and arrows by reading and through trial and error. Under his dad's instruction, Mitch was well versed in most types of firearms before he was even 12 years old, but he came to prefer the simple bow to all other weapons. He had spent so much time perfecting his technique that it was all he needed to consistently bring home game.

His dad taught him the basics of tracking as well, and like archery, Mitch spent hours studying the subject and practicing what he learned in the field. He had little interest in the methods most of the local weekend hunters used, such as ambushing deer from a shooting house situated over a planted bait field. Mitch preferred instead to do things the old way, tracking his quarry one on one in the forest and skillfully stalking to within arrow range to make his kills. His dad hadn't taken him seriously when he first began this type of hunting, but Mitch had gone on to amaze him with his success rates. Now Doug Henley readily told anyone who asked that his son was the number one hunter in the family and he didn't have to bother with it any more because Mitch kept the freezer full of game.

Most of Mitch's friends didn't understand his obsession and it sure didn't win him any popularity contests at the local high school, particularly since he didn't play football or other sports. None of the girls he developed crushes on could care less how well he could shoot a bow, but Mitch didn't let that deter him from his passion. Now things were going to be different and fast, and he wondered how those more popular kids were going to cope with this new reality. It was going to be hard for them, if not impossible, but Mitch was confident that he could live without all that stuff the solar flare had destroyed. He didn't need a car, cell phone, electricity or a grocery store as long as he had access to the woods that he was making his way back to now. It was ironic that as rarely as he was this far away from the remote Henley farm, the one day that he happened to find himself in New Orleans was the day something like this had to happen. Mitch didn't like that he was starting from such an alien environment, but he also looked at it as a test—a test of his physical strength and his wits as well as his resolve. He would pass it, because unlike the stupid tests he was forced to take in the classroom, this

ENTER THE DARKNESS

one was real and important—this one was a test where the score meant the difference between life and death.

Mitch felt better about his surroundings the nearer he got to Lake Pontchartrain. The interstate passed through an expansive area of marshlands for the last five miles or so before the beginning of the bridge, giving him a needed break from the urban surroundings he'd been traversing. He knew from consulting the map that reaching this marsh area meant that he'd covered approximately 10 miles since leaving Mr. Greenfield's house. His watch told him it was 10 p.m. He was making good time, but it was still another 15 miles to the North Shore. Mitch was determined to make it there in one long push even if he didn't arrive before daylight. He took off his backpack and sat on top of the retaining wall to eat an energy bar and drink some water. He was alone on this northbound section of roadway for now, though that would probably change by tomorrow.

Twelve

DESPITE HER WORRIES AND tossing and turning earlier, April finally fell into a deep sleep due to exhaustion and when she woke again it was daylight already. She made her way back to the kitchen first thing and after opening another one of David's now-warm Cokes, got down on her hands and knees to search for the tiny parts she'd dropped the day before. She found several small screws and some washers in the narrow gaps between the old wooden cabinets. When she laid them out and compared them to the parts list and diagram that came with the carburetor kit, April found that she was still missing a tiny spring and a small rubber washer. The only other place they could be was under the refrigerator, so she braced herself and gripped it with both hands, pulling and working it away from the wall a few inches at a time. The floor under the old appliance was as disgusting as she expected, with dust and cobwebs and pieces of insect parts that had been there since long before she and David moved in. She sifted through the filth and wiped it up a little bit at a time with paper towels, taking care not to throw anything in

ENTER THE DARKNESS

the trash before checking carefully, and at last she found what she was looking for. All the parts were back on the table now, so she pushed the refrigerator back into place and sat down to get to work.

Putting the carburetor back together was far more pleasant than taking it apart. The parts that had to be reused were clean now after the washing in mineral spirits, so she didn't get her fingers covered in grease like the day before. She took great care putting the new parts in place and aligning the thin gaskets with the fastener holes. Then she threaded in the screws that held the body of the carburetor together and tightened them as evenly as she could. There were adjustment screws on it as well, and she'd heard David talking about "idling it up" or "idling it down" and "adjusting the mixture" when he was trying to get the car running before. She figured she would have to do the same to get the motor to run properly once the carburetor was installed. She had to eat something first though, so she made herself a peanut butter and jelly sandwich from the half loaf of bread left in the cabinet and ate it while sitting there admiring her handiwork. She thought that maybe this mechanic stuff wasn't as hard as David made it out to be, but she knew too that what she'd done so far didn't mean anything unless the Mustang would run when she was finished. When she was done eating she went to the front door to look out on the street and see if anything was going on, but it was quiet at this midmorning hour. She would check on Mrs. Landry again later, but she wanted to try and get the car running first. Then she could tell her to get ready for the trip to Slidell. April hoped that would be later today, because she intended to leave without delay as soon as the car was fixed.

The instructions that came with the rebuild kit did not include any information about how the carburetor was actually installed. April took it out to the car and pulled away the rag David had put over the place she knew it went. There was a smooth metal surface with a large hole that matched the opening on the bottom of the assembled unit, and the final large gasket that fit perfectly there was obviously meant to go in between the mating surfaces. April careful put it in place to check the fit, and was relieved to see that it seemed right. She just needed to find the bolts that held it down, because they weren't in the box with the rest of the stuff he'd put in there. Why he didn't keep everything related to the project together was beyond her, but not surprising for David.

She checked the workbench and looked in all the boxes on the floor but still couldn't find them. Then she decided to check the trunk, and sure enough, there was another box in there with more parts in it, and something else she didn't even know David had—a service manual! There was a picture of the first Mustang model on the cover and the title said it was a repair manual for all Ford Mustangs from the 60's

ENTER THE DARKNESS

through 1973! April pulled the box out of the trunk and carried it inside. This was going to be a lifesaver! She flipped through the pages until she found the section on carburetor removal and then she understood what the other parts in the box were. The step-by-step instructions and illustrations showed the mounting procedure and the related parts like the air breather and cover. April knew she could get this right now, and figured David must have bought the manual before he took it off. Maybe he didn't tell her because of the price, or more likely, he didn't want her to know he couldn't figure it out without a book. Either way, she was happy to have the manual. She took care to follow the instructions to the letter and when she was sure she had done everything right, she slid into the driver's seat with her fingers crossed and held down the clutch and turned the key.

The engine spun over rapidly, but didn't start up. April pumped the gas pedal a few times and tried it again. The result was the same. She tried holding the pedal all the way to the floor and that didn't work either. It was turning and turning with no sign it was actually going to run. She was terrified of running down the battery, so she got out and looked over her work again while reading through the manual. She couldn't find anything she'd omitted, but then she suddenly remembered something else. She looked through David's small stock of oil and other lubricants and found a spray can of carburetor cleaner. She'd heard David's friend mention this some time ago when he first started having trouble with the car not wanting to start. He said if gas wasn't getting to the carburetor that a small amount poured into the intake would get it started, and that carburetor cleaner spray would do the same thing. April didn't know if David had ever tried it or not, but she didn't have anything to lose at this point. She removed the breather cover and sprayed a generous stream into the opening, hoping it was the right place. When she returned to the driver's seat and turned the key again, the old V8 engine rumbled to life! It ran rough and went dead as soon as she let off the gas, and she knew that what she had to do next was adjust the idle screw. The shop manual explained this in detail, and 20 minutes later the Mustang was running smoother than it had since she'd met David. April was ecstatic at her success. She had a ride out of here and a way to get to her daughter! It was late afternoon and only another hour until dark, but all she had to do was grab a few things and tell Mrs. Landry it was time to leave.

* * *

Mitch reached the edge of Lake Pontchartrain by 3 a.m. He was alone out there for the most part, other than when passed by the occasional running vehicle heading out of the city. None of the drivers had stopped to talk to him or offer

ENTER THE DARKNESS

him a ride though, and Mitch hadn't tried to get the attention of any of them either. Those who had operable vehicles were far more fortunate than most, but Mitch wondered how long their means of transportation would be useful in light of the problem of getting more fuel. On the farm they kept extra gasoline and diesel on hand for the tractor, his dad's boats, and things like the lawn mower. It wasn't a big supply, but there would be enough fuel to operate the old truck and the tractor for at least a little while. Mitch didn't anticipate the need to drive far, and that was a good thing because the truck needed work and wasn't used often. If he knew exactly where to find them, it would be tempting to consider driving it to Texas to get his parents, but it was unlikely the old antique Ford would make it that far without issues. Aside from that, he knew the fuel problem would probably be insurmountable. From the stories he'd heard after Hurricane Katrina, Mitch knew that people would steal fuel during a major shortage, and he doubted it would be safe to travel with extra containers on board that would be an irresistible temptation to roadside bandits.

His fantasies of making such a trip were just a way to keep his mind occupied as he walked. He was getting tired, not so much from the physical exertion, but simply from lack of sleep. The nap in the hammock at Mr. Greenfield's house had helped a little, but since he had slept so little the night before, it was catching up with him. Thinking of all the challenges that lay before him helped to keep him moving though, and now that he'd reached the bridge across the lake he felt he'd made the first milestone of his journey, as he was about to leave New Orleans behind him for good.

A light breeze blowing out the southeast carried the refreshing smell of the salt air with it, a pleasant change from the scent of oil and other smells of the city. The nighttime temperature was pleasant, neither too warm nor too cool, but perfect for walking. Just as there had been everywhere else along the lanes of the interstate, there were abandoned cars, pickups and 18-wheelers scattered here and there as far ahead as he could see on the bridge. The far shore was barely visible as a dark silhouette on the horizon, a complete change from when he'd crossed the bridge going the other way nearly 24 hours earlier. *Had it really only been that long?* Mitch was surprised at the thought. The whole world had changed in such a short time. Most people were no doubt completely disoriented and unsure what to do. That was why he'd encountered so few people on the move since he'd left Mr. Greenfield's neighborhood. He was undoubtedly one of the minority who not only had a plan, but was implementing it already and determined that nothing or no one would stop him. He felt sorry for all the folks who were going to be hit the hardest by this when the enormity of the situation finally became clear to them, but he knew there was nothing he could do for them. Maybe some of them would figure out a

ENTER THE DARKNESS

way to get through it or find someplace to go where they could survive it, but he was quite certain most would not.

Mitch stopped and took another break shortly after daylight, sitting down for a few minutes to watch the sunrise before continuing the final half-mile to the north end of the bridge. He'd made good time for the first night, and was looking forward to getting some sleep as soon as he found a suitable place on the shore ahead. As he approached the end of the bridge he saw some activity on the water near what appeared to be a marina. A couple of small boats with outboards on the back were heading out on the lake, and a larger sailboat was slowly moving away from the docks, the light morning breeze barely filling its sails. Mitch thought about what Mr. Greenfield had said about there being nowhere to go, even if he and his wife still had their boat. Mitch didn't know anything about sailing other than the little he'd read about it in books, but it seemed to him that a boat big enough to sleep on that could carry a lot of food would be a safe refuge. Maybe that was what the owner of the one he was watching now had in mind. Mitch doubted he was simply going out for a joyride.

Just beyond where the bridge ended and adjacent to the marina he'd seen, Mitch spotted an undeveloped area of a few acres of woods and marsh next to the highway right of way. He had to walk farther north to find a place to climb down over the retaining wall, and then he was finally off the concrete after all those hours. Mitch picked his way through a tangle of brush and high grass and found a dry patch of open ground hidden within a grove of scrubby pines. He took off his backpack and quiver, and using the pack for a pillow, stretched out to get some much needed rest.

Thirteen

NO ONE GOT MUCH sleep at Stacy's house that first night after the blackout. Mrs. Burns didn't make it home that day or during the long, dark night that followed. Mitch didn't show up either, and this seemed to confirm what Mr. Smith had suggested—the effects of whatever caused all of this were widespread. Stacy's mom's car was surely disabled, as was the new truck Mitch was driving. Lisa wasn't as worried about Mitch as Jason and Stacy were about their mom. Mitch could take care of himself, and Lisa had no doubt he was probably already walking in the direction of home if he hadn't found some other way to get there. He would probably come here first looking for her, but Lisa knew it was a long way to New Orleans and that if he were walking it would take him several days. She couldn't sit here waiting for him with Stacy's mom stuck in Hattiesburg. There was no way Mrs. Burns was going to be able to walk home, even though it was only about 35 miles from the hospital where she worked. Mrs. Burns was not an outdoorsy person nor was she into physical activities, so it was unlikely she would attempt it.

ENTER THE DARKNESS

"She's probably just fine at the hospital," Lisa had told Stacy and Jason numerous times over the last twenty-four hours. "Unless she can find a ride with someone who has an old vehicle that runs, she'll probably stay put. The patients are going to still need care and you know the hospital probably has generators that can run for a long time."

"They do," Jason said, "but I'll bet a lot of their equipment was fried just like everybody's cell phones were. Patients are going to die if the machines that were keeping them alive aren't working."

"I don't even want to think about that," Stacy said. "If Mom *is* there she and the other nurses and doctors will do everything they can for their patients. I'm just worried she was already on her way home. She could be *anywhere* between here and there. That's why I don't want to wait any longer."

"I agree," Lisa said. "We don't have to wait. We can leave this morning for the farm. We might as well start walking. It'll only take a few hours if we don't stop much."

"I just hope you're right about that old truck running," Jason said.

"We didn't use it much, but I know it was running fine before, and it's older than some of the other vehicles we've seen running, like Rusty's car. I don't see why it wouldn't."

"Somebody could steal it out of the barn," Stacy said. "People might start stealing vehicles that still work since so many don't."

"Yeah, she's right," Jason said. "We'd better get moving before that happens. With Mitch and your parents gone, there's no one to stop someone from taking it."

"I'll leave Mom a note on the table by her bed so she'll know where we went—just in case she somehow makes it home first," Stacy said.

"Yeah, and let's stop by Mr. Holloway's store and tell him too," Lisa said. "If Mitch comes here to Brooklyn first, he'll probably stop by the store."

"If it's open," Jason said.

"You know Mr. Holloway won't be far away no matter what. His house is right beside it." Lisa had been stopping in at the little country store for as long as she could remember. It was the only real store left in the tiny little town, and Mitch and her often went by there after school for a soda and snack before heading home. She doubted Mr. Holloway would be going anywhere. His gas pumps might not be working, but he would sell the food and other stock he had to the locals that were his friends until he ran out. Lisa knew that most of them would pay in cash anyway.

"I wish I had a way to give you kids a ride to the farm," Mr. Holloway said after hearing their plans and giving them some candy bars to take for their long walk. "You won't have any trouble walking though, I don't suppose. Just watch yourselves if you do drive that old truck to Hattiesburg. I'd recommend staying on the back roads if I were you. I've been

ENTER THE DARKNESS

talking to some of the other fellows in town, and they figure we'd better keep a watch for outsiders passing through. Folks are going to get plenty desperate when they run out of everything and realize they don't have many options. It'd be best if y'all could go get your mother and get back down there to the farm and lay low for awhile until Doug and Mitch make it back. You'll be better off out there away from all the highways and main roads."

Lisa hadn't thought about how close Highway 49 was to Stacy's house, and how that highway might soon be busy with refugees trying to find food and other things they needed. She knew Mr. Holloway was right about their farm though. It was way out in the middle of nowhere and not on the way to anything. She doubted any strangers would find their way there, and she knew that when Mitch got back he would keep a sharp lookout for intruders. Her dad had made sure they were self-sufficient living out there, and they had never wanted for anything when hurricanes and other storms knocked the power out for a few days. It would be a lot longer this time, but at least they had the land and the cows and the creek out back. They would have what they needed with or without the power grid working. She told Mr. Holloway they would heed his advice. She knew all the back roads in the vicinity of the farm and a route from there most of the way to Hattiesburg that avoided highways. It was the way Mitch went whenever he had to go there, and Lisa had ridden with him many times. She could drive the old truck by herself just fine, because her dad had taught her how even though she was far too young to have a license. She wouldn't need to though, because Jason had his license and it would be best to let him do it in case they happened to encounter any police officers once they got to the city.

They left Brooklyn on the paved county road that ran more or less parallel to the creek, walking at the pace that Jason and Stacy set. Lisa knew she could go much faster if she were alone, because she liked to run and hike and was in great shape from spending so much time doing both around the farm. She was sure Jason and Stacy were capable of walking the 15 miles they had to go, but she didn't want to push them to exhaustion. They had all day to get there, and a few hours wasn't going to make much difference one way or the other.

The road ran roughly parallel to Black Creek on the north side for the first several miles. The stream was the only federally designated National Wild and Scenic River in the state and was Brooklyn's one and only claim to fame. There was a big canoe rental operation on the main road near the bridge, and people came from all over on summer weekends to paddle the pristine waterway winding through Desoto National Forest. Lisa had thought briefly about the three of them renting a canoe and paddling downstream to the Henley farm. It would be possible, because the creek ran close to the

ENTER THE DARKNESS

back of their property and they already kept a family canoe hidden in the woods there. But then there would be the problem of having to return it, which might be difficult if they didn't have enough gas for the old truck after going to Hattiesburg for Mrs. Burns. The rental operation wouldn't be open anyway, and even if they found the owner there he probably wouldn't be interested in renting them one after what happened. The other reason Lisa thought it might be better to walk was that there was always a chance someone would drive by in a running vehicle and offer them a ride, saving them time. That's exactly what happened two hours later, when they were about six miles down the road from Brooklyn.

The three of them stopped walking at the sound of a big truck shifting gears as it came around a distant curve behind them. Lisa guessed it was an old logging truck, as there were a lot of them around here. When it came into view, they stood by the side of the road watching it approach, but they didn't put out a thumb or try to flag it down. The driver slowed anyway, and after getting a good look at them, stopped in the middle of the road just past where they were standing.

"Awesome!" Jason said. "I was already getting tired of walking."

They ran up to the cab and the man driving looked them over. Lisa didn't recognize him, and neither did Jason or Stacy, but he was friendly and after asking where they were headed, told them to climb in the cab. There was barely enough room for the three of them to squeeze in, but they made it work and the truck driver took them as far as he was going in their direction, dropping them off at the turn off to the gravel road that led to the farm.

"Thank you!" Lisa said as they climbed out of the truck.

"Nothing to it. Glad I could help you kids out. There's a lot of folks walking right now and I imagine there'll be a lot more."

The old truck pulled away, leaving Lisa and her friends in the silence of the national forest. The road here didn't pass any other houses but Lisa's, and they walked the last few miles among tall pines that grew almost to the shoulders on either side. When they reached the gate to the long lane leading to the house, Lisa unlocked it with her key and shut it behind them. It was strange walking home like this knowing no one would be there. She had no idea how long it would take Mitch to get back, but she was certain he wasn't there yet. If they were lucky, they could drive to Hattiesburg and get Mrs. Burns and make it all the way back before Mitch did. Lisa knew that would be best, because he would be furious if he got here first and found the old truck missing.

The truck was parked in the barn where it always was, and Lisa's mom's car was in the open carport attached to the house. Her dad's state patrol truck was in the side yard, and his patrol boat was under its shed next to his personal fishing

ENTER THE DARKNESS

boat. Lisa unlocked the house and they went inside. Everything was as it had been left, and there was no sign anyone had been there since Mitch and her parents left. There were kerosene lanterns and several candles on the top shelf in the pantry. Her mom kept them there for power outages during storms, and Lisa pulled them down to distribute around the house so they would have light when they got back. From what she could guess by the angle of the sun, it was early afternoon and they still had a few hours before dark.

She went to Mitch's bedroom, the one room in the house that was off limits to her any other time, to get his key to the old Ford. Since Mitch drove it much more often than his dad, she knew he kept the key in his room. She thought she would find it on his nightstand, but it wasn't there, nor in the drawer beneath. She looked on his study desk among his notebooks and other school stuff and couldn't find it there either. *Darn it! I'll bet he put it in his pocket out of habit even though he wasn't going to need it for the trip to New Orleans* she thought. She went to her dad's office next, hoping to find a spare in his desk drawer. The keys to his state game warden's truck were there, as well as an extra set for her mom's Chevy Trailblazer, but even though she searched the whole room, there wasn't another key for the Ford.

"This doesn't look good," Lisa said, as she and Jason and Stacy stood next to the old truck with both doors open, having already searched the glove box and under the mats for a spare.

"Maybe we can hot wire it like they do in the movies," Jason said.

"Yeah, but do you know how? Mitch probably does, and my dad too, but I sure don't."

"I don't have a clue," Jason said.

Lisa pondered their options as she raised the hood and looked at the engine. There *had* to be a way. They would eventually figure it out, but they were running out of time today. Even if they knew what they were doing, it was getting late and it would be best to wait until tomorrow to leave. They *had* to figure out how to crank the truck in the morning, and she was determined to do it. As they walked back past her dad's patrol truck, Jason commented on the rifle that was locked in its security rack inside. It was a Smith & Wesson M&P 15, issued to him by the wildlife department. Jason said they should get it out in case they needed it, and Lisa agreed. But like the ignition key to the old Ford, the keys to the patrol truck were not to be found in any of the places she looked in her dad's office. There were more guns in the safe, including her .22 carbine, but Mitch had apparently taken that key with him too. The AR-15 was the only weapon they might be able to get to, and that would require breaking into her dad's truck, an idea that Jason suggested.

"Maybe tomorrow," Lisa said. "Let's see if we can get the

ENTER THE DARKNESS

old truck running first, and if I still can't find a key to the gun safe, then I guess we'll have no choice."

Fourteen

ONCE SHE WAS SURE that it was running right and confident that it would start again, April switched off the Mustang and put the key in her pocket. She didn't want to waste gas by running it any longer than necessary because she was unsure of how much gas was in the tank. The fuel gauge had been broken since before David got the car, and it was always a guessing game as to how much was in it. He had gotten in the habit of keeping it mostly topped up because of that, but April couldn't be sure how close it was to full now. She just hoped it would be enough to get to Hattiesburg because from what she'd heard about other stores, buying more might not be an option. She knew the V8 engine was a lot thirstier than the 4-cylinder in her little Honda, but if there were a few gallons in the tank it would get her there.

She went back into the house and scrubbed the grease off her hands in the kitchen sink, then went next door to tell Mrs. Landry the car was running. The first round of knocking got her no answer, so she banged the door much louder, calling out her name as well. After several minutes of this,

ENTER THE DARKNESS

April grew impatient and walked around to the side of the house, where she tapped on the back bedroom window. There was still no response from inside and no sound of movement. April thought it odd since she hadn't been able to get Mrs. Landry to answer the door the evening before either. She couldn't be sleeping *that* long. Walking back to the front of the house, she noticed a partially opened curtain in a side window that opened to the small living room. It was too high above ground level for her to look inside, so April went back around to where the Mustang was and got the little stepladder David had out there. When she returned to the window and stepped up to look inside, April was shocked to see Mrs. Landry sprawled facedown on the rug in front of her couch. She banged on the window frame as hard as she could without breaking the glass and called out to her, but there was no response. Something was badly wrong, and April knew she had to get inside and find out what.

When she returned to the front door, April had the largest screwdriver she could find among David's tools, as well as a hammer. She drove the blade into the door casing in line with the doorknob lock, hoping that the deadbolt above it was not also locked. The door gave way, swinging inside with less effort than she expected, and April rushed into the living room and knelt beside Mrs. Landry. She put a hand on her shoulder and shook her gently, but there was no response. April then pushed harder to attempt to roll her over, but was surprised at how stiff she felt. Then she reached to touch the side of her neck to check for a pulse and involuntarily pulled her hand back in shock. Mrs. Landry's skin was cool to the touch. Her neighbor was *dead!*

Looking at the body, April could see no evidence of what caused her death. She wondered if she could have fallen and hit her head, but when she managed to roll her all the way over, there was no sign of a bruise or of blood anywhere. *Could it have been a heart attack or a stroke or something?* April figured that had to be it. The woman was at the age that anything like that could happen. Maybe the stress of the situation and thinking about having to leave her home had triggered it. It made her sad to think that she was just a day late getting the car running. If she could have gotten Mrs. Landry to her sister's house, maybe this wouldn't have happened. But there was nothing to be done about it now, and thinking of that, April was at a loss. She couldn't call the sister and she couldn't even call an ambulance or the police. She couldn't move the body by herself and she didn't know what she would do with it if she could. The only thing she could think of was that maybe she could find the address of the sister and stop by and let her know when she passed through Slidell. She searched through a stack of letters and bills on a bookshelf in the same room until she found it. Then she went to the bedroom and pulled a heavy blanket off the bed, bringing it into the living room to carefully cover

ENTER THE DARKNESS

Mrs. Landry's body before she locked the door behind her and left.

Before going back inside her apartment, April looked up at the rays of sunlight filtering through the tops of the nearby oaks. It was getting late and she still had to go through her things and sort out what she needed to take with her. She would need her clothes, and most of Kimberly's things as well as all of the food in the pantry and kitchen that was still good. As she thought about all this, April began to consider that perhaps it wasn't such a good idea to try and leave so late in the day. Even if she were packed and ready, she would only make it about halfway to Hattiesburg before dark. If she had trouble with the Mustang, she wouldn't be able to see to figure out what was going on without a flashlight, and she thought too there could be any number of obstacles in the road. She wanted to get to Kimberly as soon as possible, but having an accident or a breakdown in the dark wasn't going to help her accomplish that. Reluctantly, April decided that it would be best to spend the last hour of daylight sorting through her stuff and putting it in the car. She would then get a good night's sleep and leave at the crack of dawn.

Getting her stuff together turned out to be much easier than sleeping. April went to bed a couple hours after dark, but lay there tossing and turning and unable to forget the image of Mrs. Landry's lifeless body sprawled on the floor next door. Finding her neighbor dead like that and realizing there was nothing she could do about it and no one to even tell, drove home the harsh truth of the situation that was unfolding. Unable to sleep, April now wished she had gone ahead and left in that last hour of light, but now in the pitch dark that enveloped the city, it wasn't feasible at all, especially since once again, she heard distant gunfire ringing out from somewhere in the streets. She got up and paced the floor, trying to wear herself out so she would have to sleep, but that didn't work either. She went outside sometime between midnight and dawn and sat on the front steps, drinking another can of warm Coke and eating the last of a box of cereal from the pantry while she listened for more shooting.

The smell of acrid smoke from burning buildings hung heavy in the humid night air and April wondered how long it would be before troublemakers found their way to her street. The only thing she was certain of was that she wasn't going to be there to find out. She hadn't seen Jennifer at her house across the street, and although she felt bad about it in a way, she didn't really plan to look for her either. Mrs. Landry was different, because she was her next-door neighbor and elderly, and April and David had known her since they'd moved in, unlike Jennifer, who she'd barely spoken to before the blackout. Besides, since she hadn't seen her, April thought maybe the woman had already left with someone else. Now that she could do nothing else for Mrs. Landry, April was determined to leave at first light. Everything she was taking

ENTER THE DARKNESS

was in the car, and since she couldn't sleep there was little she could do inside the apartment with no lights. She kept her vigil outside until she saw the first hint of the new day, and then she locked the door to the apartment for the last time and slid behind the wheel of the Mustang.

April held her breath as the engine spun for several seconds. It almost seemed like it wasn't going to start but then she heard it fire and come to life like it had yesterday, and she finally exhaled again as her heart pounded while she waited for it to warm up and smooth out. When it did, it seemed to be running perfectly, and April pressed the clutch and shifted into first, then pulled out of the driveway and into the street. Although it was still a bit hard to see, April left the headlights turned off to avoid attracting the attention of anyone far ahead. After hearing so much shooting, she knew she was vulnerable to carjacking and that a running car would make her a target if she crossed paths with the wrong people. She hoped that by leaving at this hour she would encounter less activity on the road, in the form of other vehicles, bicycles or pedestrians.

The Mustang was running smooth and seemed to have plenty of power as she shifted into second gear before coming to the stop sign at the end of her street. She turned right to take a shortcut she always used to get to the interstate, finding it necessary to weave back and forth across the lanes to avoid all the stalled cars and trucks blocking the road. She had just pulled onto the interstate from the on-ramp when she noticed movement between the abandoned vehicles scattered in the lanes ahead, causing her to instinctively let off the gas and slow down. As she drew nearer, she saw that a man had stepped into her path in the only open lane, and was waving both hands in a downward motion, the way highway workers flagged drivers to slow or stop. April couldn't tell if the man was some kind of official or not, but he wasn't wearing a policeman's uniform and didn't appear to be armed. Her mind was racing as the distance closed. *Was he trying to warn her of some unseen danger ahead? Did he have the authority to stop or redirect her for some reason? Or was he just some random dude trying to flag her down because she had a running car and he wanted a ride?* April didn't know, but it also occurred to her that his intentions could be worse too. If she stopped, the man might try to take her car by force. If he had a gun that she couldn't see, he might shoot at her anyway, but she determined then and there that she was *not* going to stop. Kimberly was her only priority now and she knew she couldn't afford to let anything, or *anyone* stand in the way of getting back to her. She maintained her steady, but slow speed and laid down on the horn, letting the stranger know in no uncertain terms that he'd best clear the way.

Despite her actions, the man didn't move from the lane and April had to stop to avoid running over him. As soon as she did, he rushed around the car and attempted to open the

ENTER THE DARKNESS

driver's side door. April had locked both doors when she got in that morning, a practice she was in the habit of doing anytime she drove anywhere with Kimberly. She was glad she'd remembered it today as the stranger pulled at the door handle and yelled at her to open it. He was saying something about an emergency and needing help, but April wasn't falling for it. If he truly needed help he wouldn't be trying to force his way into her car. She gunned the engine and let off the clutch again as the man climbed on top of the car and began beating on the roof. He was able to cling there for a few tense seconds until she was up to 40 miles an hour and found an opening in the lanes that allowed her to quickly swerve back and forth. She saw him tumbling in the roadway in her rearview mirror when he came off and then she slowed back to a safer speed to pick her way through all the vehicles. She was wired with adrenaline now and wary of every congested spot she came to, knowing that others could be lurking most anywhere to try the same thing. But she was determined that if it happened again, she was not slowing down. That first encounter was far too scary, and she would run over anyone else who tried it before risking that again.

Despite her willingness to use the Mustang as a weapon, April managed to leave New Orleans without having to. She passed a few other people traveling the interstate on foot and by bike, but none threatened her and by sunrise, she was across the bridge and approaching the Slidell exits. She honored her commitment to stop by Mrs. Landry's sister's house, even though it meant getting off the highway and driving several miles out of her way to find it. The silver Buick that she's often seen next door when Julie was visiting wasn't in the driveway though, and no one answered the door when April knocked. The woman could be anywhere, April knew, probably stranded somewhere because she was out and about in the car the morning of the blackout. There was nothing else she could do, so April drove back to the interstate and continued on her way.

Another encounter with a group of teenagers that tried to force her off the road encouraged her to consider an alternate route. Often, when she'd gone to Hattiesburg with David to visit his parents, he chose to use Highway 11, an older two-lane route, rather than the interstate. He liked it because the traffic moved slower, and he could stop anywhere he liked without waiting for an exit. Once she'd crossed the state line April decided to get on Highway 11 herself. There were places to turn off if she needed to and she figured the likelihood of running into the wrong kind of people would be less. She was to soon find out she was wrong, however, and also that there was far less gasoline in the tank of the old Mustang than she'd assumed when she left. The car had been running great all this way, but once she was several miles out in the middle of nowhere on Highway 11, she felt it sputter, lose power, and go dead. It started again and ran a few more

ENTER THE DARKNESS

seconds when she shifted down and popped the clutch, but then it was finished. April had no choice but to steer for the shoulder as the car coasted to a stop on the desolate highway.

Fifteen

MITCH COULD HAVE SLEPT through the day if not for the annoying deer flies that woke him with their bites as the afternoon heated up. He covered his head and face as much as possible with his extra clothing, but it was so hot that way he was unable to fall asleep again. Walking in the heat of the day wouldn't be much better though, and it would expose him to more potential hassle or danger. He was pleased with the distance he'd covered that first night, and wanted to attempt to repeat it the second night, so he stayed put despite the pests. He could rest his body and feet even if he couldn't get sufficient sleep to be fully refreshed. He knew things would be better after one more night of travel, and he was impatient for the coming darkness so he could get on with it. Once he reached Mississippi, he would have nothing left but rural countryside to traverse the rest of the way home. Then he could switch back to daytime walking, and hopefully a normal sleeping pattern.

He heard voices from the nearby marina he'd seen from the bridge, but could see nothing of the activity there from

ENTER THE DARKNESS

his hideaway in the little patch of woods. All through the day the occasional car or truck passed by on the highway above, and from there too he heard the voices of other people who were likely walking like him. His thoughts went back to Charles and Deborah Greenfield as he dug one of the MREs out of his pack and sat there eating it. Now that he was actually on the road, he realized how fortunate he was to have met Mr. Greenfield when he did. He would be suffering by now without the food and water. He had no doubt he could find water, but he had no way to purify it and it would be risky drinking surface water in such a populated area. Food would be even more problematic, because although the marsh and swamplands were teeming with life, it would slow him down greatly if he had to try and hunt or fish for sustenance while keeping a low profile. The military rations weren't in the same league taste-wise as the two meals he'd had yesterday at the Greenfield's house, but Mitch knew they packed a lot of calories that would enable him to keep a strong pace. As he ate he thought ahead to the work that awaited him on the farm. He knew that as soon as he got there, he needed to take stock and get organized. His mom always kept a good supply of extra food in the pantry, especially the staple items that would keep long-term. It was just what you did when you lived miles from even a country store, and over half an hour to the nearest Walmart or other supermarket. They would be set for a long time with things like flour, rice, cornmeal, sugar and dried beans. There were all sorts of canned goods in there too, including home-canned stuff like jellies, jams, and garden vegetables, as well as jars of honey his dad bought from a distant neighbor. Having all that on hand was a good thing, because Mitch knew that getting more would be unlikely for a long time.

Water for drinking, cooking and washing wouldn't be a problem because they got all their water from a well anyway and there was a manual pump option for times when the power was out. The cattle had access to a pond and there was hay and winter feed for them in the barn. Besides that, there was always good grazing for the small herd somewhere on their 600 acres, even during the colder months that were relatively mild that far south in Mississippi. Mitch knew that butchering a steer was always an option, but he didn't expect to have to resort to that anytime soon, at least not before his mom and dad made it home. The freezer was already full of venison, though he knew it might thaw out and spoil by the time he made it home. He would kill another deer right away and make jerky with all of it that he and Lisa couldn't eat fresh. That would hold them over a long time, and there was always the option of small game or fish from the creek if they wanted something different. It wasn't hunting season, but his dad was the game warden and Mitch figured he would give him a pass, considering the circumstances.

Thinking about all this, Mitch couldn't help but look

ENTER THE DARKNESS

forward to the day and weeks ahead. In a way, it was the kind of life he often dreamed of, though that dream was set somewhere out west in a mountain wilderness and usually involved a beautiful female companion who saw things the way he did. Mitch often thought he was born a couple of centuries too late, an idea no doubt reinforced by all the stories he read of mountain men and free-ranging Indians in a time when living off the land was commonplace. He always believed he could do it if he had to, and now he was about to get the chance to prove it. The thought of not having to go back to the school was just as sweet.

His daydreams kept his mind occupied until at last the sun went down and the day faded into twilight. Mitch already had his gear sorted out and ready to go, the bow still unstrung and his quiver strapped to the pack with the arrows concealed by a shirt. Before climbing back up the embankment to the highway, he stood in the edge of the woods quietly listening to make sure all was clear in the immediate vicinity. The last thing he wanted was to be spotted and questioned by a cop or some other authority figure as he emerged out of his dark hideaway. But though he waited several minutes, no one seemed to be stirring, so he made his way onto the road and continued north.

The parts of Slidell he could see from the interstate were mostly business areas, with restaurants, motels and gas stations that were shut down and dark for the most part. He did hear the hum of a generator from an occasional building though, and here and there saw the scattered lights they powered. There were also fires in front of some businesses, and at one store Mitch could see several armed men backlit by the flames as they stood vigil over their merchandise. Although quiet a few vehicles had passed by his hideout during the day, moving cars and trucks were few and far between in the dark, and Mitch figured people were staying put at night for safety. He wondered how things were tonight in New Orleans and was glad he'd already put that part of his trek behind him. He had no doubt that the same route he'd taken the night before was much more dangerous now. Certainly many of the residents by now were coming to the conclusion that this was more than a temporary inconvenience. They would grow restless and impatient soon. Some would become desperate, and among those, many would soon become outright dangerous.

Mitch walked all night, stopping every hour and half or so to take a break and drink some water or eat a snack. He discovered that he was more fatigued from lack of sleep than he'd thought at first, and his pace was slower than the night before. He reached the long bridge over the Pearl River and Honey Island Swamp between midnight and dawn, and by an hour after sunrise he was once again off the road and bedded down in the woods, this time in his home state.

He slept better that second day and was on the move

ENTER THE DARKNESS

again by late afternoon, less concerned about being seen now that he was in Mississippi. He stayed on the desolate interstate until he was past the small city of Picayune, then he turned west by climbing down at an overpass to reach a county road that would take him to Highway 11, the old route that ran mostly parallel to I-59. Mitch had planned to follow Highway 11 for the next leg of his journey, but just before he reached it he came to railroad tracks and changed his mind. He'd forgotten about it, but the railroad ran right alongside Highway 11, separated from it by a narrow strip of woods in most places. It occurred to him that it would be a better idea to stick to the railroad. It was unlikely other people would be traveling it and no trains would be running, so he would have it to himself. He would follow it until he reached the point where it was time to turn east for the final stretch to the Henley farm.

    A full night of walking the tracks put him far from all the big towns to the south and well into the Mississippi woods he so knew and loved. Dawn brought a heavy overcast with the promise of rain later in the day, but Mitch didn't care. He found his next spot to bivouac in a dense stand of bushes between the railroad and the highway. There was an isolated farmhouse about a half-mile farther north, but it was on the other side of the road and didn't concern him. It was midmorning and he had just fallen asleep when he was awakened by the sound of a car coming up the road from the south. The engine was so loud Mitch knew it had to be an old V-8 muscle car, but he was too tired to bother getting up to look. At the speed it was approaching it would be past him in a moment and on its way. At least it should have. But just after it went by he heard the motor suddenly shut off. It was quiet for a second and then he heard the car jerk and the motor cough back to life, only to stop again seconds later. Mitch lay there waiting, hoping whoever it was would start the engine again and keep on going, but that didn't happen. Instead, he heard a car door slam. Curiosity got the better of him at this point, and he decided to have a look and see what was going on.

Keeping hidden in the bushes just above the shoulder of the road, Mitch crawled to a position that would give him a view of the highway to the north. He had seen a few abandoned cars in that direction before he stopped for the day, but the classic Ford Mustang sitting there now was new and Mitch knew it was the car he'd heard. The hood was up and whoever was driving it was hidden from his view on the other side. Mitch watched and waited, until a figure emerged, stepping back around to the driver's side door.

He was surprised to see that it was a young woman or girl, maybe even about his age, though he couldn't tell for sure because he was several hundred yards away. He could see that she was pretty though, with long, dark hair and a slim, graceful figure. He hadn't expected a female driver when he

ENTER THE DARKNESS

heard the loud car, and seeing her standing there with the hood up, he wondered what happened to cause it to die so suddenly when it sounded like it had been running fine before. He was sure she was alone after watching for several more minutes, and it occurred to him that maybe he could help her get it started. If so, she might offer him a ride since she was going in the direction he was traveling. Mitch went back to where he'd left his gear and gathered up his things. He had changed into his camo hunting clothes since he'd reached the countryside, and he hoped his appearance wouldn't frighten the girl. He figured it probably wouldn't as long as he called out to her before he got too close and didn't startle her.

He walked back to the roadside still cautious, wanting to take another look from within the trees before stepping out into the open. He was glad he did because three men were approaching the highway from the direction of the house that he'd noticed before on the other side. Mitch figured that they too had seen that the girl was having car trouble and had come out to help. If so, he would just stay put and let them handle it. A ride would be nice but there was no guarantee she would offer him one anyway.

From where he stood it appeared that one of the men was older, maybe in his 40s, while the other two were probably closer to 20. Mitch saw the three of them gather around the car and the girl, obviously talking about the problem but he couldn't hear anything that was said because of the distance. Finally, the older man got in the driver's seat after they had looked under the hood and then closed it. Mitch thought maybe they had figured out the problem but then he saw the girl backing slowly away from one of the younger men, who was approaching her near the front of her car. It was hard to tell exactly what was going on, but something didn't look right. The man kept moving in on her and then reached out to touch her as she leaned back against the hood to get farther away. He seemed to persist until suddenly she slapped or hit him, causing him to step backwards, while holding both hands up to his face. Then, as Mitch watched, he simply collapsed to the ground as if he had fainted. Mitch saw the girl run around the car opposite the driver's side as the older man got out and the younger one hesitated and then came after her.

There was no longer any doubt in Mitch's mind that these men were up to no good. The girl was running as fast as she could away from her car now, but the older man who'd been in the driver's seat was right on her heels. She was running in Mitch's direction but the man pursuing her was faster. Mitch saw him grab her by the hair before she got far and he was already stringing his bow as he watched the aggressor violently yank her off her feet. The girl fell hard onto the shoulder of the road as Mitch moved quickly to close the gap, keeping close to the roadside bushes as he quietly slipped into

ENTER THE DARKNESS

bow range, a hunting broadhead now nocked on his string.

By now the other man was catching up to join the action too. Whatever the girl had hit the first one with, it put him down for keeps, but she was still outnumbered two to one and Mitch knew she had little chance without some help. He'd never pointed a real weapon; either firearm or bow, at a fellow human being, but Mitch had no doubt of his ability to put his arrow where he wanted it to go if necessary. He had closed the gap to about 75 yards and neither the girl nor her two attackers were aware of his presence. The one that had caught her and thrown her down now stooped to pick up something she'd dropped, and from where he stood now, Mitch could see that it was a knife. The man clenched it in a reverse grip and moved in on her with clear intention and at that moment, Mitch drew his bow. There was no time to ponder the implications of what he was about to do. There was only time to act.

Sixteen

APRIL HELD HER BREATH as she turned the ignition key again after the Mustang came to a stop. The starter turned the engine to no effect until she finally gave up for fear of running down the battery. *Now what?* She was beginning to have hope she would make it all the way to Hattiesburg, until this.

She looked around before getting out of the car. The highway was a desolate scene of abandoned vehicles with no sign of life or movement. Darkening clouds to the west she hadn't noticed before promised approaching rain, and the heavy overcast did nothing to improve the mood of this lonely place or lighten her spirits at the prospect of being stranded. She had thought it safer to travel this smaller, two-lane highway, because it ran through few towns and communities, through a landscape of mostly uninhabited woodlands. Where the Mustang had rolled to a stop, she saw one isolated house set back among a grove of pine trees west of the road, and on the other side behind a narrow buffer of trees were railroad tracks that ran parallel to the highway

ENTER THE DARKNESS

about a hundred feet away. Looking closer, she could see a wisp of smoke coming from behind the house and figured someone had built a fire to cook or heat water for morning coffee. It was insane how everything had changed so fast, how modern life had ground to a halt in an instant, and people were trying to adapt any way they could. In a matter of days, most people were already reduced to near primitive conditions, camping beside their homes or in their vehicles.

April got out of the car and walked around to the front of the hood. It didn't make sense that it would go dead now when it was running fine so far. From the way it sputtered and stopped, her best guess was that it was simply out of gas. With a non-working fuel gauge, she had no way of knowing how much was in the tank when she'd left, and getting more in New Orleans was out of the question. She pulled the latch and raised the heavy hood; it's rusty hinges squeaking loudly in the silence that hung over the deserted highway. She could hear the ticking sound of hot metal from the engine as she removed the wing nut holding the breather cover to check the carburetor. She sniffed for gas fumes but didn't smell any. The car was almost certainly out of gas and she had to get more, but how? She screwed the breather cover back on and slammed the hood in frustration.

All these stranded cars around her probably had fuel in their tanks, but how would she get it out? There had to be a way to siphon or drain some, but she didn't even have a container to pour it in to refill her tank even if she could figure out how to get some out. She looked in the direction of the lone house across the road, wondering if she could get some help from the people there. She was almost afraid to go over and ask, but just as she looked that way, she saw that she wouldn't have to.

Three men had suddenly appeared from around back and it was clear they had seen her. They were already striding across the lawn in her direction at a brisk pace. April stood by the car and waited. As they got closer, she began to wish they *hadn't* seen her. She had been around a lot of rough people in the various places she'd lived, and she was usually able to stay cool in such situations, but the looks of these three didn't inspire trust, nor did they look like they belonged at a rural house this far from the city.

Just from the way they walked she could tell they had an attitude that didn't match the fear and confusion of most people she'd encountered since the lights went out. These three had the look of predators zeroing in on their next meal, but April knew better than to show fear and give them even more confidence. She stood her ground as they stepped up to the shoulder of the road from the grass. Now that they were just a few yards away, she could see that two of them were barely older than her—maybe just out of their teens but likely not over twenty-one or twenty-two. The one leading the way, though, looked like he could be forty or older. They all had

ENTER THE DARKNESS

the hard, tanned look of men who worked construction or some other kind of outdoor labor, but the leader, with his scarred face and tattoos of skulls and Rebel flags all over his arms, looked like someone who enjoyed fighting for his after-work recreation. He was the first to speak:

"Da-aaamm! What have we got here? Is that what I think it is? Is that a genuine 1969 Mustang Fastback?" The older man whistled as he took in the car. Clearly it was the kind of ride that had turned him on even before the blackout—before old relics like this were the only cars that would still run. "I told y'all it was a Ford V-8. I could hear it coming a mile away," he said, glancing over his shoulder at his companions.

"That's all right," one of the younger men agreed, but his gaze had passed over the antique car and was fixed on April. He took her in from head to toe, not caring at all that his appraisal of her body was obvious. The third one was staring, too. It was like they hadn't seen a female in a long time, even though the blackout had just happened earlier that week.

The older one turned his attention from the car back to April. "Where'd a teenaged girl barely old enough to drive get a car like this? Your daddy buy it for you, sweetheart?" He grinned as he walked to the driver's side of the car and opened the door and slid behind the wheel. April was still standing in front of the car by the hood.

"It's my fiancé's car. I think it's just out of gas. It was

running fine until now, but the gas gauge doesn't work, so I didn't know how much I had until it ran out. I was going to walk up to your house over there and see if someone could help me. If you don't have gas, there's probably some in these other cars. I just need to get a few gallons so I can get to Hattiesburg."

"What's your hurry to go up there? If this Mustang belongs to your fiancé, then where the hell is he? Don't he know it's dangerous for a pretty girl like you to be driving around out here all alone? Ain't many cars that'll run at all after what happened, and there's a lot of people that would like to have a car like this about right now. Besides, you fill up with gas here; you'll just run out again somewhere else. Don't you know the situation is the same everywhere? It ain't gonna be no different in Hattiesburg."

April was about to explain the real reason she had to get to Hattiesburg, but then she thought better of it. These men were unlikely to be sympathetic to her situation, and the best she could hope for now was that they would leave her alone and give her a chance to figure out how to get more gas herself. But she already knew that wasn't going to happen. The older man seemed to have taken possession of David's Mustang as if it were his own. He pumped the accelerator and turned the ignition key, grinding the starter as April had done, with the same result.

"Yep, I think you're sittin' on empty all right. But that ain't

ENTER THE DARKNESS

nothin' to worry about. Like you said, we can get some gas out of one of these cars. But there ain't no hurry, 'cause time don't mean nothin' no more anyway. You oughta hang around and party with us for awhile. You might forget all about that fiancé of yours that let you set out on the road like this by yourself without any gas. What's your name anyway, sweetheart? I'm Reggie, and that's my nephew, T.J.," the man said, nodding at the one who had stared at her first. "And that's his buddy, Danny," he indicated the other man, who had not yet spoken. "They ain't much older than you, and I'll bet they'd be glad to have a girl around to talk to."

"Hey, T.J., why don't y'all show her over to the house while I see if I can get some gas in this car and get it off the road?"

April said nothing, but glanced over her shoulders as the man was talking, trying not to be obvious, but looking at her options for an escape route. The situation didn't look good. Even if she could outrun them, which she doubted, if she lost the car, her chances of getting to Hattiesburg would be slim. It would take days to walk there, even from here, and that was assuming she had plenty to eat and the strength to do it. She was determined not to give up the car without a fight.

The older man was still sitting in the driver's seat of the Mustang, looking at the details, running his hand over the upholstery. "You just don't know how much I always wanted one of these back when I was a kid your age. Say, where'd you learn to drive a stick anyway? I didn't think anybody under thirty even knew what one was these days."

"Girls like her know a lot more'n you give 'em credit for, Uncle Reggie," the one he'd called T.J. said. "I'll bet that ain't all she's good at."

April backed up against the hood of the car as T.J. stepped toward her, keeping her right hand behind her, out of his sight as she waited for him to close the distance. If she was going to do anything to stop them, she had to act now and act decisively before T.J. or all three got their hands on her. Their intentions were clear, and if they were this bold right out here on the open road in the broad daylight, they obviously knew there was no one else around to intervene. If they got her inside the house, all bets were off and she wouldn't have a chance. She was determined to fight for all she was worth to make sure that didn't happen. The rules had changed, and April knew that if she was going to survive, she couldn't play by the old ones.

She waited until T.J. grabbed her by the left upper arm and pulled her in close to him. He reached for her hair with his other hand, so sure of his ability to drag her to the house with little resistance that he was oblivious of her right hand, with which she was reaching for something in the back pocket of her jeans. April felt the familiar textured grip of her Spyderco, and when her fingers closed around it, it was

ENTER THE DARKNESS

out of her pocket in an instant, the four-inch blade snapped to the open position with a flick of her thumb. T.J. was so preoccupied with thinking about what he was going to do to her that he didn't realize what was happening until it was too late.

April twisted her body beneath him and brought her knife hand up between his arms and straight to his unprotected throat, where the short blade could do the most damage with the least amount of effort. When she felt the serrated edge meet soft flesh, she sliced as hard and deep as she could, almost losing her grip with the force of the effort. The effect was immediate. The man staggered back and clutched at his wound, trying to stem the fountain of blood spurting between his fingers while his brain was still able to process the shock of what had just happened. April quickly stepped back and around to the passenger's side of the car, putting more distance between herself and his companion, who was momentarily paralyzed with disbelief. But then the other one screamed "T.J.!" as he watched his friend collapse to the ground and then turned to her with fury in his eyes.

"STAY BACK!" April shouted, holding the bloody knife in front of her as she backed toward the rear of the car to gain more distance before he could rush her. "I'll cut you, too, if you don't leave me alone!" He hesitated for a moment, unsure what to do, as he was unarmed and clearly shocked by what she'd done to his friend, but then she heard the car door slam as the older man got out.

"Get her, Danny! Don't let her get away!"

April turned and ran as the younger man rushed her. She had enough of a head start to sprint past the rear of the car before he could get around to the passenger's side, but the older man was right behind her, chasing her down the highway. He was much faster than she had imagined. He caught up with her before she had covered thirty paces, and grabbed her by the hair as he overtook her. She tried to slash at him with the knife, but he yanked her off balance before she could connect, causing her to drop her weapon as she fell hard onto the gravel shoulder. She rolled and twisted to get out of his reach. Her fingers closed around a handful of the small rocks that she was determined to hurl in his face as a last resort. She saw him bend over to pick up the knife she'd dropped, and it was clear that he intended to do to her exactly what she had done to T.J. But then something really strange happened. . . .

The man suddenly fell for no apparent reason, collapsing to the roadway beside her when his knees buckled beneath him. She couldn't understand what caused him to fall, but after he was down, she saw blood pooling on the pavement beneath his body. The other attacker, who had caught up and stopped to watch as she was grabbed and thrown to the ground, turned to run back in the direction of the car, terrified by something he'd seen. But before he could reach

ENTER THE DARKNESS

the passenger side door, he too collapsed. It made no sense to April, who hadn't heard a thing, but then she saw something bright standing out in stark contrast to the black of the second one's T-shirt where he was thrashing facedown by the car. The strange object was just to one side of his spine, where the kidney would be. Blood was welling up around it and spilling onto the road just as it was around the older man who had fallen. It was then that April recognized the bright object for what it was: the tail end of an arrow, with a fletching of bright yellow feathers.

April scrambled to grab her knife and then quickly got to her feet. Her hands were scraped from the hard fall onto the gravel, but she put the pain out of her mind as she looked around for whoever had taken out her attackers with, of all things, *arrows*. When she looked back along the highway in the direction toward New Orleans, she saw a lone figure step up to the pavement from the high grass in the ditch, holding what could only be a bow. The figure was dressed from head to toe in hunter's camouflage, and if not for his movement, it would have been impossible to spot him against the backdrop of bushes.

The archer was walking her way, and April's first impulse was to turn and run. But she knew if he wanted to shoot her, running wouldn't do any good. She told herself that if he wanted to kill her, he would have done it before revealing himself. She stood her ground, determined that if he did shoot her, it would not be in the back.

Her four-inch knife was little better than nothing against a weapon that could kill from afar, but the adrenaline from using it on the first attacker still coursed through her body. *Had she really cut a man's throat?* She had felt the resistance of flesh against the edge of the blade, and there had been a fountain of blood as he staggered back. *But was he really dead?* If he was, he was on the ground in front of the car and she couldn't see him from where she stood. She glanced at the other two and was sure that both of them were dead. The one hit in the back had thrashed for a few seconds but was now still.

As the archer approached, he raised one hand in a friendly wave and removed the floppy camouflaged hat that shadowed his face. She could see that he was smiling in a way that she took to be an attempt to reassure her. He called out to her, saying he would not hurt her. Although an arrow was on the string at the ready, he carried the bow loosely in one hand, down by his side in a non-threatening way. She waved back and tried to return the smile, lowering her knife as she did but still keeping her grip white-knuckle tight as she waited for him to get closer, her next course of action totally dependent upon what happened when he did.

About the Author

SCOTT B. WILLIAMS HAS been writing about his adventures for more than twenty-five years. His published work includes dozens of magazine articles and twelve books, with more projects currently underway. His interest in backpacking, sea kayaking and sailing small boats to remote places led him to pursue the wilderness survival skills that he has written about in his popular survival nonfiction books such as *Bug Out: The Complete Plan for Escaping a Catastrophic Disaster Before It's Too Late*. He has also authored travel narratives such as *On Island Time: Kayaking the Caribbean*, an account of his two-year solo kayaking journey through the islands. With the release of *The Pulse* in 2012, Scott moved into writing fiction and has written several more novels with many more in the works. To learn more about his upcoming books or to contact Scott, visit his website: www.scottbwilliams.com

Made in United States
Orlando, FL
29 January 2024